RED ROOM:
New Short Stories Inspired By The Brontës

Edited by A. J. Ashworth

UNTHANK BOOKS

First published in 2013
by Unthank Books
www.unthankbooks.com

Printed in England by Lightning Source, Milton Keynes

ISBN 978-0-9572897-3-4

Edited by A. J. Ashworth

Cover artwork by Rachael Carver
Typeset by Tommy Collin

A percentage of the proceeds from this anthology will be donated to The Brontë Birthplace Trust, Thornton, Bradford. Many thanks to all the writers who have kindly contributed work for no fee in order to support the Trust.

Contents

Red Room: New Short Stories Inspired By The Brontës

Emily B

Too much rain
in the blood. Too much
cloud in the lungs.

One summer in ten
a dry wind rushes the moor.
I find you

pegged to the skyline,
green dress in a wild dance,
hair flying east,

mouth wide open, wanting
to gulp down a cure,
breathe it

right to the core.
But bad water
leaches the graveyard,

drains through the bones
of mothers and fathers
into the well,

into your cup.

Simon Armitage

Introduction

The Brontës. Our nation's most famous sisters – Charlotte, Emily and Anne. When we think of them we think of the moors, of great affecting narratives such as *Jane Eyre*, *Wuthering Heights* and *The Tenant of Wildfell Hall*, we think of lives cut short and talent lost (Emily died at the age of thirty in 1848; Anne at twenty-nine just a few months later; Charlotte at thirty-eight, whilst in the early stages of pregnancy).

Their lives had by then been marked by tragedy: they lost their mother and two older sisters in childhood and their beloved, but troubled, brother Branwell died just a few months before Emily and Anne in 1848.

It is no surprise then that these tragedies had a deep effect on their writing – and it is possibly because of such great personal losses that the universal themes of death and love the sisters explored in their stories continue to resonate with us today.

The Brontës fascinate us. We love their books, we love the films and television dramas made of their books (well, some of them) and we love them. The parsonage at Haworth, where the sisters lived from 1821, draws around 70,000 visitors every year from all over the world, including a large number from

Japan which, as a nation, seems to be as much in love with them as we in the UK are; it even has its own Brontë Society. But the sisters were not born at Haworth. It may come as a surprise to some to learn that they were in fact born in Bradford – in a village called Thornton, in a cottage which, despite undoubtedly ranking as one of the top literary birthplaces in the country, even the world, is not under any kind of protection. In fact, 72/74 Market Street, Thornton, in the heart of West Yorkshire's Brontë country, has had a rather unstable past: it has been a restaurant and a private residence and, from the 1990s until 2007, was restored and opened as a museum by the crime novelist Barbara Whitehead before she sadly had to sell it on. More recently the property was in receivership and there are plans currently for it to become a coffee house.

And this is the reason for this anthology.

Towards the end of last year (2012), I was added into a group on Facebook: The Brontë Birthplace Trust. They had only recently formed and were looking for ideas to raise funds to help them one day buy the house and to also help them promote the village as a tourist destination. They are also hoping to hold a year-long exhibition in 2015 to celebrate two hundred years since the Brontës arrived in Thornton. I suggested a short story anthology and was encouraged to take the lead on it… and, so here it is.

The writers who have written the stories here have done so without receiving a fee and I heartily thank them for contributing and supporting the work of the Trust. A percentage of the proceeds from sales of the book will be donated back to the Trust by Unthank – and I thank them for that act of generosity also. In the anthology, you will find a poem by Simon Armitage as well as twelve new stories – all inspired by the Brontës, their lives, their work – written by some of the best short story writers in Britain today. There are new stories based on *Wuthering Heights* and the characters in it, those about imagined meetings between Charlotte and her loves, both real and imagined, an invented correspondence between Jane Eyre and another famous literary heroine, a feminist re-writing of one of the most famous Brontë chapters and many more – but in all of them you will notice Charlotte, Emily and Anne lingering among the branches of words and ideas contained within… the three of them continuing to provide inspiration to writers to this day, almost two hundred years after they were born in that small Bradford village.

In Chapter Two of *Jane Eyre*, the heroine is locked in the deathly red-room as a punishment for being unjustly accused of fighting. The fears aroused during the course of her imprisonment, of ghosts and dead men 'troubled in their graves', stay with Jane and cast a long shadow over the book.

With this *Red Room*, I hope you will not want to escape but instead to enter and stay willingly: but for now… 'Here pause: pause at once. There is enough said.'

A. J. Ashworth
May 2013

Stonecrop

Alison Moore

'After all, she was a sweet little girl.'
– Emily Brontë, *Wuthering Heights*

After the picnic, Catherine walked home. Mr Blakemore did not like to see young ladies running, sweating, unkempt. She walked slowly, coming into the kitchen without a trace of perspiration, without a lock of hair unpinned, with a little bunch of bright yellow flowers still held in her fist. She arranged the flowers in a small vase before answering her mother's question. Her mother had to say again, 'Catherine, where is Mr Blakemore?'

Catherine had first met Mr Blakemore one day the previous summer. Her mouth was still sticky from a small cake she had made at school that afternoon and had then eaten out of a Tupperware tub on the way home. She found Mr Blakemore standing in the doorway of her mother's house. He hesitated before stepping backwards so that Catherine could come inside. He asked what she had in her mouth. Catherine showed him her tub of cakes and said that she had made them in Domestic Science. 'Cookery,' said the man, happily inspecting the cakes before glancing disapprovingly at Catherine's crumby mouth, her tacky lips. He did not, she discovered, like to see young ladies eating in the street, nor eating much at all.

Even after he married Catherine's mother, he was never a 'love' or a 'darling' or even 'Derek' or 'your father'; he was always 'Mr Blakemore'.

There were many things, Catherine discovered, that Mr Blakemore did not like. He did not like to see her standing still and daydreaming. He did not like her to speak in a voice any bigger than *this* – he held his thumb and forefinger millimetres apart to show her how small her voice should be. He liked her always to have a smile on her face – he placed two fingers under her chin, lifted it and waited for her to show him her smile. He did not like the way she left the breakfast table, her knife chopped into the block of butter like an axe stuck in wood.

He liked to see her sewing. He liked to see her in a dress. He liked her to sit next to him in church every Sunday, where she was to raise her head when she sang, to open her mouth *this* wide – he put four fingers and his thumb inside her mouth so that she would not forget. He liked her to pack up a picnic for them to share when he took her into the countryside, where he sat with his binoculars to his eyes, telling her what he could see. He told her what wild flowers were growing at the cliff edge.

After the picnic, Catherine came home alone. She did not run, spattering mud up the backs of her legs, breaking a sweat. The skirt of her dress was not flying; her hair was not undone and streaming behind her. She walked slowly, putting her wild, star-shaped flowers into water before saying to her mother, 'He had an accident.'

Catherine was given sweet, black tea. She was required to talk about what had happened, but she could not remember very much, and that was, said her mother, said Catherine, because of the shock.

Catherine insisted on visiting Mr Blakemore, who remained in a coma, but she hoped that he knew she came and that he could hear her. She went weekly, religiously, and spent the hour at his bedside, talking to him in a voice no bigger than *this*, no more than a whisper coming from the pretty lips she held close to his ear, a little smile lifting her face.

Ashton and Elaine

David Constantine

1

Ashton – not his real name, but even supposing he ever had a real name, nobody in this story knew it – Ashton was found behind Barmy Mick's stall late afternoon on a Saturday in the week before Christmas, as the market closed. Mick's son Kevin, a boy of eleven, found him. He went to fetch some sheets, boxes and sacking, to begin packing up, and when he lifted the tarpaulin, under which they were kept dry, there lay Ashton, shivering. Kevin covered him up again and went to tell Mick. Dad, he said, there's a coloured lad under the tarpaulin. Mick took a tilley lamp from a hook over the stall, and with it, drawing off the covering, illuminated Ashton, who lay on his back with his eyes wide open. Fetch your mam, said Mick. She was soon there. All three then, father, mother, child, stood looking down at Ashton in the light of the lamp. Day was ending in a drizzle. The lamp had a haze, a tremulous mist, of light around it.

Ashton wore a stained, thin jersey, stained, thin trousers that were too short for him, unfastened boots that were far too big. No socks, his bare ankles looked raw. He shivered, and stared upwards. The mother, Alice, bowed over him. What you doing there, love? she asked. Ashton, who was perhaps Kevin's age, said nothing. Mick handed the tilley to Alice and knelt down. What's your name, son? he asked. Again Ashton said nothing; and it was not possible to tell, from his expression, whether he understood the question or not. He seemed to be clenching himself tight, as though trying not to shiver, and his face perhaps showed only that: the effort, and the failure. Mick stood up. I'd best go and fetch somebody, he said. Alice handed the lamp to Kevin, kneeled, drew one of the packing cloths over Ashton, up to his chin, and laid her hand on his forehead. Ashton closed his eyes, perhaps – who knows? – to safeguard a kindness behind his lids. But he could not stop shaking and his face, which, eyes shut, looked more exposed than ever, still manifested the struggle.

Mick came back with a policeman. Alice stood up. Kevin shone the light over Ashton. The policeman squatted down, removing his helmet and cradling it between his big hands in his lap. Ashton opened his eyes. Can you talk to us, sonny? the policeman asked. Can you tell us how you got here? The rain came on heavier. Ashton said nothing, only stared, and shook, the thin cover showed it, crumpling and twitching. Better get him moved, said the policeman, rising, putting on his helmet, turning aside, speaking into his walkie-talkie. Alice knelt again, rested her hand on Ashton's forehead. He closed his eyes.

The ambulance, first the siren then, in silence, the twirling blue light, drew attention to the scene behind Barmy Mick's stall. A score of people assembled, keeping their distance, in a half circle, all gazing, none speaking, two or three held lamps, in which the rain shone. The ambulance men, in their uniforms, were as imposing as the policeman. One knelt, Alice moved aside, he drew off the cover, and in a murmur asked questions, which got no answer, meanwhile feeling over the child's limbs and, very delicately, under his spine where it rested on the sacking. The other removed his loose boots – so bruised the feet – and with great care the two together slid him over on to the stretcher laid by. Then they lifted him and walked the ten paces to the ambulance's wide-open doors, Kevin following with the boots. The doors were closed. Slowly, quietly, the ambulance felt its way out of the market. At a distance the siren began to howl. Everyone dispersed. The last shoppers went home, the stallholders resumed their packing up.

2

The consultant on duty at the Infirmary that afternoon was Dr Fairfield, a paediatrician, a local man who, on the way to begin his shift, had called at the maternity hospital to see his daughter who had just given birth to her first child. The sister in charge undressed Ashton, still speechless, staring and shaking, and stood back, watching Dr Fairfield's face. Many times she had watched him assessing the state and the immediate needs of a child; and on the way home and sometimes in the night when she thought of her work, she saw the child in question, or perhaps a whole series of them, all hurt, all harmed, all distinct in *how* they suffered, but as the register of that, almost as the accumulating sum of it, she saw Dr Fairfield's face when he first kneeled to be at the same height as a child standing before him or looked down closely from above at a boy or a girl laid on a clean sheet on a trolley. And now as he contemplated Ashton, the sister saw something like puzzlement, like wonder, in his eyes. Many years in the job, he looked, to her, in the case of Ashton, to be being pushed to the edge of his knowledge and comprehension, to a sort of frontier, beyond which lay only a wasteland devoid of any human sense. Unspeakable, he muttered. The boy stared up at him and shook as though under the skin he was packed with raddling ice. And still his face looked tormented by the effort not to shake, as though if he shook it would be the worse for him, but to halt the shaking was beyond his strength. Among the marks on his body, those on his wrists and ankles, of shackling, were perhaps, being intelligible, the easiest for the eyes and the mind to bear.

A trainee nurse came to the door. The sister kept her away and brought her message to Fairfield that the police were in reception. Tell them I'll come down when I can, he said. But it won't be soon. They'll want the clothes and the boots, I suppose. And could you ask her to find Dr Adegbie? Ask Dr Adegbie will she come up, please. Then he turned back to Ashton, spoke softly to him, rested a hand on his shoulder and began to study what had been done to him and what a doctor might be able to do to mend it.

3

Back then disappearing was a lot easier than it is now. You walked down a street, took a bus, sat among travellers at a railway station, unfilmed. Of course, children who were reported missing would be looked for by the police and sometimes also by the general public in organized search parties; but the unreported missing, why should anyone look for them? And a child who, as in Ashton's case, arrived from nowhere, speechless, unless he was on a list with a photograph or a description or sketch of what he might look like – and Ashton, the police ascertained, was not on any such list – how should a place of origin be found to return him to? The two scant bits of clothing and the cruel boots said nothing. The police labelled them and put them in a cupboard in a plastic bag. And at the Infirmary Ashton was given, first, pyjamas and later, when he could walk, clothes that fitted him comfortably so that in his outward appearance he did not look odd among the other children on the ward. He walked well enough, in a hunched and hesitant fashion, but he did not speak, though the doctors found his speech organs to be healthy. He had, moreover, keen hearing and very sharp eyes. But he would not speak. He watched. 'Watchful' was the word that came to mind whenever a doctor or a nurse remembered Ashton in the Infirmary. He was easily frightened; he had resources of terror in him that on unforeseeable occasions suddenly might be broached; but his usual state was watchful, his eyes looking out in a restless wariness.

4

The peat and gritstone country even today, crossed busily by trunk roads, motorways and flightpaths, surveyed unceasingly by satellites, if you once raise your eyes to it from the west side or the east, it will lie in your dreams and in the imagination high and level ever after, as a foreign zone, as a different dimension of the life of the earth. The cities for more than two centuries with blackening labour pushed up into it, climbing its streams, and the ruins are up there still. In the cities the moors feel very close. In the age of the smogs you might not often have noticed them, but the smogs are a thing of the past and from railway platforms now or from high office windows, look out east or west, you are bound to notice that the moors are there. You are very close to a zone and a form of life in the world which under the human traffic and the human litter goes down and down many thousands of feet, unimaginably dark, unimaginably old, and with not the least memory or presentiment of love or pity.

In 1850 a mill-owner by the name of Ferris did the usual thing and built himself a mansion outside town high above the dirt and the noise by a stream that had not been spoiled and with the open moor accessible from his garden through a small back gate. The house, which to please his wife Mr Ferris christened Astolat, was of the local stone whose appearance for a while was light and sparkling. But the smoke Mr Ferris had hoped to escape came up there on the wind, some days the very air had a bitter taste, and Astolat blackened in the look it gave to the world. Between the wars, when the mill was done for and the family went bankrupt, the Local Authority acquired it cheap, changed its name to Hollinside, and used it first as a convalescent home for men whose lungs had been ruined in the mines and the mills, and then, after the Clean Air Act, as a children's home. Quite soon the rhododendron leaves no longer dripped soot whenever it rained, the women no longer wiped the lines before they hung the washing out to dry, and the children, taken for hikes across the moor, no longer blackened their hands when they scrambled on the crags. The stone of the house stayed black, but upstairs and downstairs the many rooms let in the light through generous windows, the tiles and cladding of the conical towers reflected every weather, all indoors was brightly decorated, and the spacious sloping and terraced gardens received the southern and the western sun. The brook, steep-sided, was fenced in safely for its passage through the grounds; but the tones of voice of it, soft or ferocious as the weather dictated, lingered in the dreaming memory of the children long after they had grown up and gone elsewhere.

When Ashton came to Hollinside in the latter part of January 1963 the stream was utterly hushed in ice under feet of snow. That winter had begun in earnest on Christmas Eve, deep snow, a hardened ungiving earth, week after week, the birds dying in thousands. Hollinside, warm and cheerful indoors, stood in a scoop of frozen stillness, from where, tracking the stream, very soon you might have climbed on to England's backbone, three hundred miles of it, the long uplands, snow on snow on snow, under bright cold sunlight, bright chilling starlight, and the visitations of blizzards out of blackening skies on a wind that cut to the marrow of every living thing. Ashton, never speaking, looked enchanted by the snow. Warm and safe, the bustle and chatter of the room behind him, he was seen standing at the window, viewing a silence that perhaps, after its fashion, seemed to him kindred to his own. The wariness went out of his eyes when he contemplated the snow. He watched the frozen powder of it falling in sunny showers from the trees when the birds, small handfuls of imperilled warmth, swooped on the crumbs thrown out for them on the cleared flagstones.

Fuel and food, the doctor, the nurse, the workmen, the visiting teachers, came up to Hollinside after the snowploughs out of town. And twice a week, Mrs Edith Patterson was brought down early from Lee Farm on the moor, by her husband, Fred, in his truck, to help with the meals. She met Ashton on a Friday – he had been at Hollinside three days by then – and on the way home that evening she spoke about him in tones which caused Fred, driving very cautiously through the banks – almost a tunnel – of snow, to glance at her often. There was an excitement in her voice, and she seemed, as she talked, to be trying to understand why meeting Ashton was so important. He doesn't speak, she said. And it's not that he can't, it's that he won't. And when Fred asked how he made himself understood, she had to think about it. I don't rightly know, she answered. I don't recall that he smiled or nodded or shook his head. But he takes everything in. His teachers are sure he's learning. When he's upset, he starts shaking. But when he feels all right, he looks at you like you were a blessing on him.

Night cannot fully descend over fields of snow. It seems to hover, quivering, lit from below. The farm lights showed. The dwelling made a brave appearance, its barns and byres and useful sheds clustering round. Elaine stood watching at the big kitchen window, her gran, Edith's mother, holding her shoulders and also, above her, looking out. As the truck drew in and halted on the crunching snow, Elaine waved her right hand.

5

After the blizzard of 24th January the roads were impassable. Edith could not get to Hollinside, nor Elaine to school. The stillness around Hollinside deepened. Ashton stood at the window looking out. How immensely blurred all the outlines were! The ground fell away in soft undulations over terracing and steps. Mrs Owen, the Matron of the home, came and stood by him. He looked up at her. She saw that he was tranquil. She smiled at him, he looked away again at the vast soft forms of snow. Seeing him there, two or three other children came to the window, so that Ashton stood at the centre of a small group. And nobody spoke. Tranquilly the children and the Matron regarded the stillness which overnight, by a silent fury, had been enlarged and intensified. Thinking about Ashton later, when he and the snow had gone, the Matron felt a sort of gratitude, she felt gladdened and encouraged by him, because she was certain that in him then, in the hush after the snowstorm looking out, some hope had started in the life that he kept hidden.

Four days after the blizzard, Ashton's teacher, Miss McCrae, rode in shotgun, as it were, on the first snowplough to get through to Hollinside. She noticed a change in him – nothing very concrete or easily describable, more like a shift of light over a surface of ice, snow or water. He did not speak; but a keener alertness and a more trusting openness had come into his face; and his movements, of his hands especially, were quicker and more expressive. She told him about her adventurous journey up to Hollinside, and seeing him so attentive, she chose her words very precisely. Soon after midday she was to ride down again, the snowplough in the meantime having pushed on to some of the outlying farms, Lee Farm among them, clearing a way. Leaving, Miss McCrae did as she had often done before. She took a sheet of white paper and wrote in a clear hand: Goodbye, Ashton. I will see you again the day after tomorrow. Two things happened. First he nodded and smiled. And on that unprecedented sign Miss McCrae would have ridden down between the ten-foot walls of snow on a high of happiness. But more happened. Ashton did more. He took the pen out of her hand and below her message, quickly and neatly, he wrote: Goodbye, Miss. I will see you on Friday. Then he gave her back the pen, bowed his head, clasped his thin shoulders and shook as though all the cold of the moors had suddenly entered him.

The big yellow snowplough came lurching up the drive. The children crowded to the windows to watch Miss McCrae climb in and be carried off. Passing through the hall, she told the Matron what had happened. He can write, she said. And very fluently. It was his secret. And now he is terrified because he has given himself away. The Matron hurried to the schoolroom. Ashton was not there. Arlene, who hadn't wanted to see the snowplough, it frightened her, said that he had run off and Miss Roberts had gone after him. He was upset, Arlene said. He was making a funny noise. The Matron found him in his bed, Miss Roberts standing over him. He had drawn the blanket up over his face, gripping it very tightly. Nothing could be seen of him except his black knuckles. But the blanket itself, tugged and convulsing, gave the two women some idea of the thing possessing him.

Edith came in next morning, having missed her usual day because of the snow. They told her about Ashton's sudden writing and what it had done to him. Though he sat at the breakfast table with the other children, Edith saw that he had withdrawn into himself. He would not let anyone see into his eyes. Of course, he was by no means the only child ill at ease. Across from him sat Albert, continually making faces, but as though for himself, as though in some private place he were trying them out, all he could muster, until he might hit on one that would have the power to placate the world. And three places along from Ashton there was Barbara, who never stopped muttering, never stopped cocking her blonde head this way and that, listening, as it seemed, to arguments about herself, harsh judgements and harsher, and her in the middle, listening, defenceless. But all that day Edith watched Ashton. And when Fred came to fetch her and with infinite care very slowly drove home through ravines of snow, she said she had been thinking about it again, she felt so much better lately, and would he come in and see Mrs Owen with her tomorrow, and talk about Ashton?

Next morning, early, Edith in her canteen apron and Fred in the dark suit he wore for all solemn occasions talked to Mrs Owen about Ashton. It would be company for Elaine, Edith said; and remembered she had said this last time when they went through the whole procedure, all the forms, and pulled out when a boy might have come to them, her nerve failing. I'm better now, she said. And added, into the pause in which Mrs Owen considered them, Aren't I, Fred? Fred nodded, took her hand, and nodded again. When he's better, said Mrs Owen to Edith and Fred, why don't you take him up to the farm for a day? See how he likes it, see how you all get on.

They left it at that. But when Fred came back again in his work clothes to fetch Edith at five, Ashton was standing in the big bay window, looking out. Their eyes met. Fred nodded, smiled, and raised his left hand in a greeting like that of an Indian chief who comes in peace. I'll swear he nearly smiled, he said to Edith, driving home.

6

Towards the end of February then, the freeze still looking set to last for ever, early on a Saturday Fred and Edith fetched Ashton out to Lee Farm, for a visit. Edith sat in the back with him and about halfway home, as he stared in his silence into the climbing and winding narrows of packed snow, she told him in a few words, to prepare him, about Elaine. He faced her at once, very close, so that she felt abashed and almost fearful that by her tone of voice and her words, only a few quiet sentences, a child could be so instantly and wholly rapt into such attention. It was as though he could see her daughter in her eyes. She patted his arm, and pointed through the window at a sudden gap and a perspective over a vast tilt of snow on which showed traces of drystone walls and, far off, there stood a house, the limitless bare blue sky curving over it and behind it. That's where Elaine's dad was born, she said. He only moved to Lee Farm when he married me.

[21]

Elaine was watching for them at the window, with her gran. She waved in great excitement as the truck halted. Getting out, Ashton was hidden from her and he kept between Edith and Fred coming into the house. Edith felt the silence deepening in him. She ushered him ahead into the big warm stone-flagged kitchen. And then it was as though the adults vanished, that is how they remembered it later; they stood back and aside and were not there, only the children were, Elaine in her best dress, a soft dark blue, short-sleeved, her left arm ending at the elbow in a bulbous flipper, her face, under black abundant curls, of startling beauty, hesitant, fearful what this newcomer would make of her, this stranger, the black boy from nowhere who would not speak – he stared, he widened his eyes looking into hers, for a long while, so it seemed, but not that he was considering her, weighing a verdict, rather that she was flooding into him, through his eyes, into his silence, and when, as it seemed, the look of her had filled him, then, very foreignly, as though this were the custom in a faraway long-lost other country, he closed his hands, crossed his arms against his breast, and bowed his face out of her sight.

You've been baking, Mother, said Fred. Edith undid Ashton's duffel coat and hung it up. Elaine snatched hold of his left hand in her right. Come and see, she said. I know you don't talk, but Mam says I talk enough for two so we'll be all right. Come and look. And she dragged him out of the room.

7

A few days later, sitting in the schoolroom at a desk with Miss McCrae, Ashton reached across her for a sheet of paper and a pen, and wrote: Elaine showed me through the window where she went sledging. Then her dad said he would come out with us if we liked. So the three of us went out. I wore my new wellingtons in the snow. Elaine's gran made a cake. Elaine's mam said I could come again if I liked. Elaine's dad said would I help him with the sheep? They are having a bad time in the snow. Here we feed the birds. – He wrote quickly and neatly but with a pause between each sentence during which, deep in his throat, he made a sound which at first was like the low insistent working of a small engine, and then more like a purring, a humming. The letters he made were not at all pinched, flattened or cramped. They were rounded, well-shaped, and making a word he joined them fluently. When I watched them forming, Miss McCrae said to the Matron afterwards, it felt like watching him breathing. His letters are airy.

Anxious that, as on the first occasion, Ashton might fall into a horror at what (and now so much more) he had disclosed, Miss McCrae hid her feelings under a brisk teacherly manner. Good, she said. Ashton, that is very good. And now I'll tell you what we'll do. She fetched a light blue folder from the cupboard and on it, in black capitals, she wrote: ASHTON'S WRITING. So all your work goes in here. He looked at her. His lips were pressed tight shut; but, beginning to be able to read his eyes, she believed she saw triumph in them, a fierce and precarious triumph. She held open the folder; he laid that first sheet in it. I will see you again on Tuesday, she said. Perhaps you will have more to write about by then.

Driving back into town for her next pupil, Miss McCrae recited the sounds that Ashton had made. Pace, pitch, rhythm and tone were all variable, which made for a great expressiveness. She improvised on a few of the possibilities. It pleased her best to begin quite high, in anxiety, move lower into exertion and concentration, settling then into contentment, a purring contentment, the lips tight shut, the tongue quite still, the humming and purring of contentment, in her throat.

8

Miss McCrae could not reach Hollinside on the following Tuesday and nor, the next Saturday, could Ashton be fetched for his weekly visit to Lee Farm. Quite suddenly, in the first days of March, the thaw came and the sound of it, almost at once, was the roaring of flood. Under its carapace of ice and its muffling of snow the stream through Hollinside enlarged its bulk and soon became visible through fissures and abrupt collapses as a dark thing mottled grey and white, battering every impediment loose, ferrying all away, breaker and bearer in one, deeper, faster, more destructive and cluttered by the minute. From above, behind glass, adults and children, equally spellbound, watched.

The moor let go its dead. The trees that, tough as they were, could not withstand three months of ice, they died inside, they stood only as skeletons, gone in the roots, not holding, and the ice that had killed them, becoming water, broke them effortlessly and as mere flotsam, draggled with other life, delivered them downstream. Beasts came too, the bloated ewes, and the small stiff lambs evicted out of the womb into the snow, with bloody sockets, eyeless, they came down swirling any way round and any way up, and a long-legged colt, or somebody's dog or cat, and once, swelling monstrously, a cow, hastily the moor got rid of them. Half a shed came down, a ladder, fencing, a chicken coop, any one of which might clog a bridge so that things nobody wished to see lodged there publicly for days. The lanes themselves, as their packed snow dissolved, became fast tributaries into the bigger rivers, the Irwell, the Tame, the Etherow, the Goyt, that now, afforced, finally could heave their effluent and torpid sludge thirty, forty miles into the sea.

Ashton watched. Among others or alone if he was let, he stood at Hollinside's big windows, watching. And at nights, closing his eyes, still seeing what he had seen, he listened to its roaring; for nearly a week the melt roared near below him, by his side, with sudden particular cracks and poundings, a clatter at times, a grating and once a sustained long undulating shriek. When he slept it was the motor of his dreams, he surfaced out of sleep and still it roared, he sank again, dumbly comprehending it.

Then the fury was done with. The stream through Hollinside became its former self, a modest thing with a low and amiable voice, and over it, that first early morning of quietness, louder than it, the birdsong started up that had been held back for weeks, the first singing of birds after a winter that had killed their kind in thousands, they sang and sang on the threshold of spring in the echoing pearl-grey, silver-grey, rosy-grey light. The stream made a pretty tinkling, running quickly and almost out of sight between its accustomed banks and over it, early morning, early evening, the surviving birds made a triumphant din of song. Along the slope, under the big windows, ran tidemarks of the stream's few days and nights of violent aggrandizement, lines of leavings, some of them hideous, some ugly bits of junk, torn remnants of birds, little sodden cadavers, which the caretaker and his two sons cleared away in sacks into a skip so that the children shouldn't see them. But Ashton, the watcher, had.

9

Towards the end of April Ashton moved to Lee Farm. He had a room of his own next to Elaine's at the front of the house looking out miles over the moorland and down towards the valley and the vast conurbation. The room was light and neat and would have been their second child's, had he lived. Ashton still went down to Hollinside for lessons with Miss McCrae on the days when Edith helped with the meals. But he slept all his nights at Lee Farm. On three further days Miss McCrae or another teacher came to him there. That was where he lived.

After tea, Ashton and Elaine shut up the chickens for the night, and brought in the eggs. He helped Fred usher the cattle in through the muddy yard for the evening milking. He learned quickly, they were soon used to him, he flitted among them, watchful, settling them. Then he stood to one side, the cows snuffled and clattered, the machine hummed, Ashton attended. He takes it all in, Fred told Edith. I never saw a lad look like that. You'd think I'd let him into wonderland. And on Saturdays, warmly kitted out, he rode on the tractor with Fred into the top fields, to see to the sheep. Fred halted, Ashton jumped down and tugged a bale of fodder off the lifted pallet behind, leaving it where it fell. The sheep came running, they raised a great noise. Ashton climbed up again, to the next drop. When all that was done, Fred left the tractor and he and Ashton went together over a stile out of the green fields into the open moor. On the north slopes the snow still lay, very bright in the sun against the drab grass and heather. The wind felt chillier in the open. They found three dead lambs and left them lying. All their wool and flesh, the small body of them, would be gone soon. They'd be clean bones, disconnected, scattered. Fred strode off, Ashton keeping up the best he could, and halted, looking down into a snow-filled hollow. The snow had shrunk since his last visit, but still nothing showed that was any concern of his. Across the snow, from perches on the gritstone, two carrion crows regarded him and the boy. They're the ones, said Fred.

Elaine asked her mother, How old is Ashton? Nobody rightly knows, was her answer. About your age, I'd say. So he could be going to school like me? Could be, said her mother, could be. Elaine did her homework at the big kitchen table while her gran and Edith got on with things. Ashton sat opposite her, drawing or writing. At first his humming and purring were a wonder to her. She didn't know what to think of it, so she had nothing to say about it either, only stared at him. But soon she got used to it, bowed her head over her work and sometimes, very quietly to herself, made a humming of her own.

Ashton drew a drystone wall with a hogg-hole through it, in great detail, all the clever fitting of the stones, and behind the wall rose the moor, and on the skyline, larger than life, sat two crows. And in his airy flowing script, with long pauses between each sentence, he wrote: Elaine's dad doesn't move his arms when he walks. He keeps them still by his sides. He stoops a bit. He goes up the hill at a steady pace. I have to run to keep up with him. He says when he was my age he was always out on the moors. He knew every rock and every stream. He says when it's a bit warmer he'll take me up there with Elaine. Then he'll teach me all the names.

Elaine looked at Ashton's writing upside down. It's better than mine, Ashton, she said. Whenever he saw Miss McCrae she opened the sky blue folder and he put his new work into it.

Once, Elaine's homework was to learn a poem by heart. It's quite a sad poem, she said. But Mrs Entwhistle says it has compassion. Elaine read two lines silently, then looked away from the book and said them aloud. Ashton watched and listened. You could test me, she said, if – Unbidden, he came and sat next to her, on her left side, so close their bare arms touched. With the index finger of her right hand she pointed

[27]

along the lines of verse. Their heads inclined together over the words. Then, unbidden, he covered the poem with his left hand. She looked up and in a poetry voice said:

> When I sailed out of Baltimore,
> With twice a thousand head of sheep,
> They would not eat, they would not drink,
> But bleated o'er the deep.
>
> Into the pens we crawled each day,
> To sort the living from the dead;
> And when we reached the Mersey's mouth,
> Had lost five hundred head.
>
> Yet every day and night one sheep,
> That had no fear of men or sea,
> Stuck through the bars its pleading face,
> And it was stroked by me.

Ashton shook his head, disclosed the text, she studied it, he covered it, she tried again. In that way she got the poem by heart and recited it to the company over tea. Ashton helped me, she said.

After that, some evenings when she had done her homework, she fetched one of her old reading books, sat Ashton by her on her left side, and pointing along the lines read aloud to him in a clear and schoolmistressy voice. Well? she said. He nodded solemnly. It's hard to tell with Ashton, she said to her mother. He's a quick learner, her mother answered. But perhaps he knows it already, said Elaine. Best assume he doesn't, said her mother. Besides, it won't hurt to learn it again.

Elaine's class were given a project: Memories. They had to ask one or two grown-ups, the older the better, to remember things, happy or sad, childhood, going to school, getting a job, getting married, good times and bad, and you had to write them out in your English book, perhaps with photographs – or, better still, if you could, make a recording of the person remembering aloud. Fred bought Elaine a small tape-recorder and said she should ask her gran to talk about growing up in the city when Queen Victoria was the queen.

Elaine practised on her mother, to get used to pressing the right buttons and saying, Recording now! This was at the kitchen table. Ashton watched and listened. Where did you and Dad meet? she asked, in a professional sort of voice. At the British Railways Club in Gorton, Edith answered. At a dance. Then there was a silence. Ashton and Elaine looked at Edith. Go on, Mam, said Elaine. You have to say more than that. You have to talk. He came down off the moor, said Edith, looking for a wife. And he found me. Was it love at first sight? Elaine asked. Edith leaned over and pressed Stop. Mam, you're blushing, said Elaine. Go and ask your gran things, said Edith. She's a better talker than me.

A couple of evenings later Elaine called Ashton into her room. She was sitting on the bed. Listen, she said. She pressed Play. Her gran's voice started, the accent very pronounced; it was her somehow brought closer, the tone of her, almost too clearly her, and only her. She was saying, Your mam had no father growing up. She was only eighteen months when he was killed. She only knew him in photographs and what I told her about him which wasn't much. My father looked after her quite a bit. He'd come to our house for tea every Friday. Gramp, she called him. He always went through the market on his way and she'd be waiting for him on her scooter at the bus stop. He bought her oranges. They were in a brown paper bag in a shopping bag and she hung them on the handlebars of her scooter. Then she went on ahead of him. She come in round the side, shouting, Mam, he's here! Mam, he bought me some oranges! Elaine pressed Stop. She looked up at Ashton. His eyes were very wide, his lips were pressed tight shut.

10

Every year on the Sunday nearest to 12th July, weather permitting, the family went for a picnic on the moor, for Fred's birthday. That year the sky was a cloudless blue. Fred, as always, invited Edith's mother. You coming, Mother? he said. Fine day, you'll enjoy it. And she always said, It's your day, Fred. You three go. I'll stay home, thank you very much. But she baked a cake which they took with them as part of the picnic. So the day had its ritual. But that year there was Ashton. You four go, she said.

They parked in the usual place just past the Boggart Stones, mid-morning, hardly any traffic, no one else on the moor. First things first, said Fred. And he took out the spade and the sack. Back then nobody thought you shouldn't help yourself to a bit of peat if you wanted to, for the garden, for potting. Still Fred didn't like to be seen doing it, which made Edith laugh. He strode off up into the moor, into a black rift he thought of as his own, where the peat was thick and firm and where from the road he was invisible. Edith stood by the truck getting everything ready. Sunhats, she said. One each, snow white. Elaine grabbed Ashton's left hand and hauled him away, past Fred, digging, his sack already beginning to be bodied into shape by the rich black after-life of plants, the layered seasons, the compacted goodness. The children ran off. You know where we'll be, he shouted. He watched them climbing away, his surviving child and the foundling, dwindling away and above him over the rough terrain. He saw, and then faintly heard, a lark rising over them. He wished they would turn and wave, but they were intent on the climb, so small already and diminishing further, the girl a dot of sky blue, the boy a dot of red. Once he saw her stumble. Ashton was on her left side then. Fred saw her reach for him – she must have seized the sleeve of his shirt with her flipper fingers, steadied herself – and they went on, until, in the hillside, a soft ravine of peat took them out of sight. He knew the ground, every character and variation of it, as well as he did every syllable of every word of the language of his daughter's body, the growth of that vocabulary year upon year as she shaped herself to live with, and become ever more dextrous, agile and expressive despite, the born deformity. But not till they reappeared, scampering higher, did he resume his digging.

On the rocky knoll the children turned and waved down to the truck, Fred heaving in his sack of peat and the spade, Edith standing by with the hamper till he should be ready to help her with it up to the picnic place. She waved and Fred did, and the children, on cloudless blue, waved back again, semaphore of love across the sunny slope, its textures of black and brown and many greens, its vigorous yearly renewal through the blonde dead grass, the bracken unfurling, the scent-dizzy bees in the heather, the black groughs, gold gorse, soft white cotton grass and, from where the children stood, the untold acres of ripening bilberries. Looking west from up there you can see the trig point on Broadstone Hill, turn south over the reservoirs to Featherbed Moss, east gives you Wessenden and the grains and the brooks that flow into it – so you might triangulate the Pattison family's happiness that sunny day. And north, over Broadhead, Rocher and Black, over Butterly, Warcock and Pule, by moss and hill, on and on, to the north you might open it more and more and forever.

Ashton and Elaine

That night Elaine was woken by Ashton crying out. It was sounds, not words, but sounds such as she had never heard from him before, terrifying, utterly confusing her, so that for a while – too long – she did not know where she was or even who she was that she should be hearing cries of that kind. She jumped out of bed, ran from her room and was hurrying to fetch her mother – but saw that his door was open and, in the light from the landing, that he was sitting up and covering his face with his hands. Seeing that, to be an immediate help, she went in. Ashton, she said, it's all right. There's nothing the matter. You're all right. She stood by him, leaned over, he uncovered his face and she saw the depths of terror that had been in hiding behind his hands. You're all right, she said again. I'll fetch Mam and Dad. But he closed his two hands on her hand that barely emerged from the left sleeve of her nightdress, enfolded the bulb and the slewed fingers in his warm grasp, shook his head, again and again shook his head, shook through and through, she sat by him on the bed and could feel him shaking as though all the cold of all the long winters of earth had taken possession of him. He would not let her go to bring help from a grown-up person. She sat with him, old as him, till his shaking lessened, his eyes in hers, her eyes in his, he watched himself better out of hers, she saw it happening, his terror being evicted. Sat, watched, till he was quiet and he let go her hand. Then abruptly he lay down, closed his eyes, slept.

Next morning he gave her a sheet of paper on which in his airy and flowing script he had written: It was only a bad dream. Even when you are happy you can have bad dreams. Please don't tell your mam and dad. Elaine read it, nodded. OK, she said. Then she added, Ashton, why won't you talk? It'd be more fun if you talked.

11

Six weeks later Edith was ironing in the kitchen. She had her back to Ashton. He sat at the big table, drawing. In summer Edith liked to iron by the window, for the light. And she was watching for Fred coming home with her mother and Elaine. Silence, but for Ashton's humming and purring as he worked; and that was an accustomed sound, like the crackle, sighing, sudden collapses of the fire in winter, or the chickens scratting around in the yard, accustomed, one ingredient, only occasionally singled out for particular thanks, in her own reassurance. Then suddenly, from behind her: Mam? She stiffened at the shock of it, but held steady, looking out through the window at a row of geraniums in pots along the south-facing shed. She *would not* look round. Well? she said, taking another of Ashton's shirts from the basket and laying it out on the board. Mam, he said again, in an accent as though he were flesh of her flesh, Mam, our Elaine says if I start talking I could go to proper school and you and Dad would let me go in on the bus with her. Elaine doesn't know everything, Edith answered, over her shoulder, ironing his shirt. It's not up to us to say if you'll go to proper school or not. But if I start talking? Well it certainly won't happen without you start talking. So the sooner you start the better, in my opinion. She reached for the next thing, a pair of his shorts. Our Elaine says you and Dad'll take us bilberrying this Sunday, he said. Very likely we will, she answered. I can read, you know. All the books Elaine gave me, I can read, he said. I should hope you can, said Edith.

The truck pulled into the drive. They're back, Edith said. Only now did she turn to him. She saw how he questioned her face. Don't shut up now, love, she said. Not now you've made a start. Then your dad and I will ask about school.

12

On Saturday 23rd November Edith took her mother to the market I called Ashton after, where he was found. Many Friday evenings Edith's grandfather, coming round for tea, had brought her oranges from there; and many Saturdays, as a child and until her marriage, she had gone there with her mother. It was the best market on that side of town, worth the trip. So two or three times a year, for a treat, mother and daughter drove down from the moor.

Barmy Mick – the third (at least) of that name – was the star of Ashton Market. His wife backed him up with teas on the row behind, and his son – a Kevin, a Jack, a Keith, a boy of eleven or twelve as he always seemed to be – helped out at the front until he grew sick of it, till he really did think his dad was barmy, till it embarrassed him scurrying among the women with their purchases; and then he vanished and was replaced by another son who looked much like him. Going back two or three times a year to Barmy Mick's, however old you got, you might well feel some good things last for ever and will never change.

Mick's customers were all women. He faced them over his trestle tables, over mounds of ladies-wear, in the sun when there was any sun, under the awning and lit by tilley lamps in the seasons of rain and cold. In frocks or macs, in hats that might be as fancy as Easter bonnets or nothing but thin plastic bags, they stood there wanting him to make them laugh.

Edith and her mother stood on the fringes, but were soon enfolded into the midst as other women came and went. Barmy by name, he was shouting, barmy by nature, and as my missus tells me twenty times a week, You get much barmier, they'll take you away. So buy 'em while you can, ladies, not three, not five, not ten, it's fifteen pairs I'm offering and the socks to match, any colour you like so long as it's red, black, yellow, purple, puce, lime-green or orange, and all fluorescent, and I'm not asking ten quid, I'm not asking five, God help me, mother, I'm not even asking two pound ten, call the yellow van now, I'm asking one pound seventeen and six, for the fifteen pairs and the socks to go with 'em, match 'em how you like or go for the contrast, each foot different, suit yourself, give the old bugger a treat, it's Saturday night. That lady over there, son, that lady who looks like Audrey Hepburn, fifteen is it, madam, and the socks just as they come? And Alma Cogan, just behind you, thirty, did you say? Take that lady thirty, Kevin, and here's the socks, it's Saturday night, give the old bugger a heart attack and off you go out and find yourself something younger.

Audrey Hepburn was standing near Edith. She had a friend with her, more a Diana Dors. It's his last chance, she was saying. If this doesn't perk him up I'm off with the butcher. Kevin pushed forward with her purchase in a paper bag. One pound seventeen and six, missus, he said. You're sure they're all in there, sonny Jim? Kevin shrugged. Count 'em if you want, he said. Audrey Hepburn did, holding them up. Kevin waited patiently. Puce goes nicely with black, he observed. Edith was watching him. That must be the lad who found our Ashton, she said. Her mother nodded. Very like, she said. Kevin moved on to the blackly bouffant Alma Cogan, and already Mick was calling him back. Leave them ladies alone, he shouted. Thirty pairs over here, another fifteen over here, Brigitte Bardots, both of 'em.

Edith drew her mother away, out of the crowd. It was starting to drizzle. You wanted some of your ointment, Mother, she said. And I thought I'd get some chrysanths. And then we'll have a cup of tea. But she halted on the outskirts, watching the boy dash in and out of the pack of raucous women, his father's patter accompanying and directing him. He ran to and fro, quick as a ferret, bringing the purchases, taking the money, giving change out of a soft wallet on his hip, a nifty boy, shrewd and grinning, self-possessed too, with a sort of reserve in himself, as though he were thinking this won't last for ever, one day I'll be off. Still Edith hesitated. Should I not tell him who we are? she asked. Tell him our Ashton is doing well and say thank you for finding him? And Mick, and his wife who does the teas, should we not go and say thank you for looking after him and fetching the policeman and the ambulance so that he got seen to quickly and came to us? Edith's mother shook her head. Best not, I'd say, she said. The less we go back there, the better, in my opinion. Have a cup of tea, if you like, then you'll have seen all three of them, where it started. But don't go introducing yourself. That would be my advice. The less talk about our Ashton, the better.

Raining again, ladies, Mick was saying, and twenty-six shopping days to Christmas. Kit yourselves out now for the festive season. Fifteen pairs for one pound seventeen and six and the socks to match. Look very nice indeed under the mistletoe in a paper hat. Mick's your man for the Christmas spirit. All good stuff, all handmade, all guaranteed to give lasting satisfaction. One pound seventeen and six! As my better half never tires of saying, They lock 'em up when they get like you, our Mick. Nowhere cheaper in the whole North West, except maybe Liverpool, and what woman in her right mind goes traipsing off to Liverpool?

Kevin dashed again through the crowd of women, towards Edith and her mother on the fringes. Edith looked hard, to remember him, she took in his intentness, his sharp canny eyes, the quickness and confidence of all his movements. When he was close, he caught her looking at him. She smiled at him, Thank you, Kevin, she said under her breath. And with her mother she turned and left the market.

Bonnet

Carys Davies

It's early when she boards the London train – dark when she leaves the house and still dark when she arrives at the station in Leeds and enters her compartment and nods to her fellow passengers.

What do they see, her fellow passengers?

They see a small, plain, obscure woman in a black travelling outfit, on her head a large funnel-shaped bonnet, also black, with a dark grey lining – a small, plain, obscure-looking woman who has been to London several times before and has no plan when she gets to her lodgings to do anything differently from the last time or the time before that or the time before that.

It's only the next morning when she is walking along Gracechurch Street that she decides to do it – and even then it doesn't feel like a decision, it feels like she is being carried along on a wave of something she cannot help.

For a long time she stands there before going in. She knows that in a great many ways she has led a sheltered life and that there are plenty of things she doesn't know, such as the right places to go for certain things. Even now, when she comes to London, she feels most of the time like a clumsy traveller in a foreign land.

She can see herself in the glass: her black travelling outfit, her big dark bonnet with its grey lining; her reflection very clear in the sparkling window.

How clean the window is!

She herself has been doing a lot of cleaning lately. When she can't write, and these days she cannot seem to write a single line, cleaning feels like a good productive thing to do.

Still not quite knowing what she'll do when she gets inside, she pushes open the door.

He wants to talk to her, he said in his letter, about her next book. The appointment is at four o'clock which means she has two hours.

As soon as she's inside, the bell on the door ringing out its last chimes behind her, she knows why she's come.

The choice is bewildering.

'That one,' she says, pointing, after much deliberation over the possibilities, and takes the money from her purse. A huge amount, it seems, for such a thing. And then she takes off her bonnet, and puts it on the counter and watches it being taken away through the curtain, and sits, and waits till it's ready. She feels naked, without her bonnet; almost asks if there is one she can borrow while she's waiting.

At a quarter to four she leaves the shop, her bonnet back on her head, and makes her way along Gracechurch Street and from there to Cornhill to attend the meeting that is due to take place at four with her young publisher.

He has written her a letter, her tall, dark-haired, handsome young publisher, but she has not received it.

Not the letter asking if they can meet to talk about her next book.

Another letter, a second letter.

It was early when she left home yesterday and climbed into her compartment, first at Keighley, then at Leeds, and she has not received this second letter, as he had expected she would have, before her visit.

A second letter in which he's told her the news that he has fallen in love with a Miss Elizabeth Blakeway and is engaged to be married.

He is standing behind his desk when she is shown into his office, a collection of papers in his hand.

His pale complexion is flushed from his morning ride in the park, and in the half-second it takes for him to look up from his reading, she takes him in afresh: his rangy, athletic height, his youthful, generous, intelligent, shrewd and sensitive face.

Never, in her whole life, has she been as conscious of her own appearance as she is at this moment – and she is always *always* acutely and painfully conscious of her own appearance when she is with him here in London, here in his office or having dinner with his mother and his sisters, or out in public, at the opera, or at an exhibition or at some terrifying literary party; but she has never, ever, been as conscious as she is now of her own tiny body and large, ill-proportioned head, her crooked mouth and her thin hair, bulked up with its little pad of stuffed brown silk – of her big nose, of her spectacles, of her age, or of how, until this moment, she has never appeared before him in anything other than black or grey.

It is pink, the new lining of her bonnet – a lustrous, pearly pink like the interior of a shell, and it is the worst imaginable thing, when he looks up, for him to see it; for him to see this small plain woman, his friend, with this unexpected bonnet on her head.

For a moment he is speechless – all he can do is stand there looking at her and wishing that he could tell her something, the future perhaps – that before she dies in eighteen months' time, at the age of thirty-eight, she will marry and be so happy, eventually, in this brief, late marriage with her quiet clergyman husband, that she will not care if she never writes another word; but he knows nothing of her future – nothing that could come now to her rescue or to his, and all he can do is to move towards her and shake her hand with what he hopes is all his usual warmth and invite her to sit, and for an hour they talk about her books, and the books of other people – they have always got along so well together, their discussions have always been so lively and full of interest – and he says nothing about the bonnet and neither does she but it is the worst imaginable thing for her to sit and feel the bright new silk around her face, like a shout, and see how embarrassed he is, how he can't look at it.

It's late when she boards the night train – dark when she leaves her lodgings and arrives at Euston Square and enters her compartment and nods to her fellow passengers. By six the next morning she is a world away, in Leeds, and by seven in Keighley again where, unable to face the prospect of being collected in the Haworth gig, she begins at once the long walk home, keeping her eyes down to avoid her reflection in shop fronts and the windows of houses. It has been raining though, here in the north. There are puddles everywhere, and she is in all of them: a small, plain, obscure-looking woman in a black travelling outfit, on her head a large funnel-shaped bonnet, also black, with a dark grey lining.

Brontësaurus

David Rose

We took an Emily apiece, my wife and I – she choosing Dickinson, I Brontë – Emily being her mother's name, she being of American descent. That's how it started, my little project. But much later.

Originally it was simply to remind ourselves of our respective homes after my first posting marooned us far from both. We would read to each other by the kerosene lamp as the svelte dark crowded in, contrasting and comparing, finding remarkably similar depths of visionary spinsterhood in our respective Emilies.

I sometimes wonder, even now, whether it was simply the draw of a kindred spirit, or the actual influence of one spirit on another – coincidence or cause? – as my wife embarked on a slow retreat into her own quasi-spinsterhood. I put it down at first to sunstroke, a diagnosis made hastily by the resident medic which I allowed to remain unrevised; it simplified things, still does. The climate – the incessant blue skies, the pinching heat – supplied useful alibi to not a few of the expatriate community.

[43]

Brontësaurus

So the deepening of my wife's twilight and the blue whiteness of the skies drove me deeper, more committedly, into the
moss-cool salve of E.B.'s world. I could taste the fog, burn my
tongue on the frost, close my eyes to the implacable blue and
see rain-hazed horizons, lovat moors. Against the swift shut-
tering of night I conjured purple gloaming. Pouring my wife's
post-tiffin cocktail, which she would nurse unsipped, I would
incant against the creak of the fan such lines as:

> But if the dreary tempest chills
> There is a light that warms again

or

> Moonless bends the misty dome.

As my wife drifted further from me on the gentle tide of solitude, I determined, then offered, to turn down the next posting, forego promotion, return home to native climes, normal-
ity. The offer was met with on her part by her then habitual
response, that of profound indifference. So we stayed, sweat-
ed it out, but less literally – successive promotions brought us
nearer to the amenities of civilized life, to the extent that the
electric current became only intermittently random. I felt I
was at least contributing a degree of outer repose to balance
her inner.

Lines from a Dickinson poem my wife had read me a world
earlier now joined the stock of Brontë lines:

> The Soul selects her own Society
> Then – Shuts the Door –.

I found a perverse comfort in those words: that my wife perhaps saw herself as an elect of one rather than a neglected
one was some balm to my conscience.

I appear to digress but necessarily so. This was the background to my own solitude, my soul's selection of E.B.'s society, my nightly haunting of those moorland retreats. Whole poems osmotically charged my memory; I would find myself whispering them as we sat over coffee looking into the dark.

I noticed in doing so how certain words recurred from poem to poem, becoming talismanic to me as they appear to have been for her. *Drear* was one, in all its variants. Related by root, surprisingly, to *blood* and *gore*, it evokes almost the opposite, a wan, anaemic mournfulness in keeping with Yorkshire fog.

Chill was another, sometimes doubled; likewise *bliss*. And *withered*, both adjective and verb.

So began my intentionally time-consuming project of tracking those key-words, like deer spoor, through the corpus. As fellow ex-pats assiduously did the month-old *Telegraph* crosswords, so I devised a crossword of my own, mapping out the tracery as exhaustively – and exhaustingly (it helped my insomnia) – as I could.

I noted down alphabetically such talismanic words, then compiled a list of every recurrence, by poem and line, that I could find. Then I widened the remit to every noun and adjective used in the body of her work. A thesaurus, then, a concordance, one could say, similar to Cruden's but on a smaller, secular scale.

As it took shape over the months, progressed through the alphabet from *agonised* to *wreath* I suddenly hit on the modestly but still absurdly ambitious idea of actually publishing the results. There were, I knew, small academic presses devoted to such amateur scholarly output. It sounds in retrospect ridiculously egotistical; I didn't intend it as such. On the contrary, it was more a sharing of the fruits of my labours, offering fellow readers of the poetry an accessible linguistic profile, an identikit as it were, of Emily Brontë. I even thought up a possible title, half-humorous, half-diffident, to mark the lightness of my pretensions.

But beyond that, on a personal level, it was simply a staking of my claim, a strengthening of spiritual ties, until my return upon retirement, to my native land.

Then came the dousing thought that such a thesaurus might already exist. I consulted what catalogues I had to hand: Foyle's, Blackwell's... Then, this being the dawn of the Internet Age, asked a colleague with such access to conduct an online search. All of which, to my relief, yielded nothing. I began the process of typing up.

My most recent promotion had upgraded me to a level of seniority that entailed deputizing, as occasion demanded, for the Commercial Secretary, in welcoming and entertaining the trade delegations of other countries. It was not a task I was fitted for, and my solitary pursuits made me even less fitted. But I gave it my best endeavour.

One such delegation that fell to me was of Japanese businessmen anxious to extend their country's share of the burgeoning Information Technology ware, as it was then known. I accepted the challenge, ordered a supply of *sake*, arranged to have it warmed. As to putting them at conversational ease I was, despite their impeccable English, at something of a loss. I knew little of their business, less of their land. 'To put them at ease, you have to be at ease yourself; talk about what you know, what you love' had been the Secretary's breezy advice.

I acted on it. As my wife cradled her cup of *sake* in the corner, I mentioned those features our native lands might have in common: rain, frost, dew-damp moss, deer tracks across fresh snow... I quoted a couplet of E.B., maybe two, to ward off the silence, then out of politeness explained their context, began to elaborate on Emily and her background. I was cut short.

'You think in our country we have not heard of Emily Brontë? You assume us to be ignorant? You have not heard of the Brontë Society of Japan?'

I had to admit I hadn't. Flustered, I embarked on an account of my personal involvement, the sense of nostalgia she spoke to, something I felt they could understand, mentioned in mounting embarrassment my little project. They seemed to perk up at that. They asked how long I had been working on it. 'Oh, years,' I replied.

They laughed. 'This could have been accomplished in days, hours.' They proceeded in turn with a detailed explanation of the computer technology that could be used for such a task, automated procedures of scanning and searching, lexical profiling... I was lost from the start.

They asked if I thought there was a call for such a thesaurus. I said I believed it would have its use, but for me the value of it was in the accomplishment, the patient tracking, stanza by stanza, as a way of losing myself in the poetic undergrowth. I voiced the thought, without much forethought, that to do it mechanically would be like a hunter using napalm, an angler explosives, a mountaineer a helicopter. They appeared not to get the point, and I began instead to talk of the rumours of a compound golf course.

Later, having delivered them safely to the Secretary, I sat over the last of the *sake* puzzling over the appeal E.B. could have to an alien culture; of whom would this Japanese Brontë Society consist? Romantic teens? Middle-aged geisha-widows? Would the appeal lie in the poetry or merely translations of *Wuthering Heights*? How much could either mean to those without the shared reminiscences of minster yards in fog, moorland drizzle? Perhaps, I thought, that was just the appeal – that of the exotic; an ironic reversal that made me smile, then forget the whole thing.

Several months later, however, a package was brought to my house, delivered to the compound by international courier. There was a card attached to an inner package. It read simply:

To an esteemed colleague.

I opened the inner. It contained a smallish book, newly printed, judging by the scent, and of academic standard: hardback, dust cover, footnotes. The footnotes were in Japanese, the text in English.

The cover read simply:

A Concordance to the Complete Poems of Emily Brontë.

Professor Atori Hakagawa.

The flyleaf was signed.

One stanza in particular runs through my brain these days:

There's a certain Slant of light,
Winter afternoons –
That oppresses, like the Heft
Of Cathedral Tunes.

There's a certain solace to it, every afternoon. I sit here, in widowed retirement, reciting it – I realize – aloud to myself over my third cocktail, which has its own parasol against the implacably blue Arizona sky.

The words are by, yes – Emily. But Dickinson now.

A Child of Pleasure

Rowena Macdonald

Even though I had made an effort with my appearance, as soon as I saw the Fenchurch family home, I felt very small and dowdy. Thirty-two Leinster Square was in one of those sweeping Regency terraces in Notting Hill that look like they're made of royal icing. The height of the house, the whiteness of it, the massive columns either side of the large front door would have intimidated even the most confident visitor, and confident is the last word anyone would use to describe me.

The brass lion's head doorknocker reflected my face back with bulbously distorted eyes so I looked even more anxious. I edged my hand up to the ring between the lion's jaws and rapped four times. After five minutes, the door was opened by a middle aged woman wearing tortoiseshell-framed glasses. She was much taller than me.

'Mrs Fenchurch?'

'Liza? A pleasure to meet you. Do call me Sally.' Our palms pressed together; mine damp, hers cool and dry, and she gave me a measured smile. Her angular body was draped in knit-wear of an expensively indeterminate shade somewhere between taupe and ecru.

'Come through... Jemima's in the telly room, probably watching some utter rubbish but she knows you're coming... would you like a drink?... Peter and I are already on the G and Ts...' Mrs Fenchurch wafted me through large rooms filled with modern art and modern flower arrangements, down to a basement kitchen of marble and steel, where a man, presumably Mr Fenchurch, was lounging at the dining table with a G and T and the FT.

'Liza, this is Peter.'

'And this must be Liza Frost.' Mr Fenchurch leapt up, sandwiched my outstretched right hand in both palms and beamed. 'How wonderful to meet you at last.' He was shorter than his wife and comfortably rounded: unlike her, good living had obviously caught up with him, but his eyes were as shrewdly intelligent. They were both City lawyers. 'So good of you to take on our wayward daughter.'

'Oh no... I'm sure she's –'

'Drink?' He held a bottle of Tanqueray aloft. 'Or a glass of wine?'

'No... I... er... just a glass of water...' I wanted to keep my wits about me, not be lulled into a false sense of security. Mr and Mrs Fenchurch might be friendly now but if their precious Jemima didn't pass her A-level English any gin and tonics I had consumed would be used as evidence against me.

Sally steered me out of the kitchen, glass in hand, ice cubes tinkling. Peter bumbled behind. Hysterical American voices screeched through the closed door at the end of the hall.

'Darling, Liza's here.' Sally pushed the door open.

Reclining on a Chesterfield in front of a huge flat-screen TV was an incredibly pretty girl in a red mini-skirt and a black off-the-shoulder crop-top with the word NERD printed on it in neon yellow. She knelt up holding her iPhone in one green fingernailed hand, flicked back a swathe of blonde hair from her face, and held out her other unpainted hand to me.

'Hi, Liza.' She blazed a perfect set of perfect teeth. Her rather small blue eyes swept from my sensible shoes to my serviceable haircut but her smile did not waver.

'Hello, Jemima.'

'Where do you want to have your lesson, darling?' asked Mrs Fenchurch. 'Down here or up in your room?'

I hoped she might suggest her room: one of the most interesting aspects of tutoring is seeing pupils' private spaces.

'Down here. I can't be arsed to go upstairs.'

'Don't use words like that in front of Liza.' Mr Fenchurch picked up the remote from where it had been flung among an iPad, a pot of green nail varnish, a hairbrush and a packet of jelly babies. 'If you're going to stay down here you'd better turn off this nonsense.'

'Da-ad, I just wanted to watch the end. Amber's been arrested.'

'What are you watching?' I asked.

'Teen Mom.'

'Half-witted brain-rot.' Mrs Fenchurch snatched the remote from her husband and cut off in mid-tirade a fat-faced girl holding a baby.

'Mo-om.' Jemima slumped then turned to me and smirked. 'Mum hates it when I call her that.'

'Yes, I do. Now, shall we go through what needs to be covered...' Mrs Fenchurch proceeded to explain the A-level English curriculum, flicking smartly through Jemima's course folder to illustrate her points. I nodded as she spoke and did not mention that I already knew everything she was telling me. It was easy to imagine her in a boardroom, frightening people with her heartless efficiency.

'How about we leave Liza to it?' said Mr Fenchurch, eventually. 'I'm sure she's *au fait* with what needs to be done. She is a full-time teacher after all.'

'Yeah Mum, just go.' Jemima rolled her eyes at me and I smiled back as conspiratorially as possible without conveying too much disloyalty to her mother.

When her parents had gone Jemima dropped back onto the Chesterfield, picked up the nail varnish and began painting her other hand. I took out my books, papers and pens, set them neatly on the coffee table and perched on the edge of an armchair.

'I know *Villette* is not as exciting as Teen Mom but we'd better start. We've only got an hour and a half.'

'*Villette*.' Jemima paused, brush in mid-air. She rolled her eyes again, but she was still smiling socially as if we were at a dinner party. 'It's so long. I wish there was a film version. Have you read it all the way through?'

'Of course.'

'Do you like it?'

'Yes.'

'I suppose you would say that.'

'Well, it doesn't matter whether I like it or not. The main thing is that you've got to study it.'

After her first lesson, Jemima preferred to receive me in her attic bedroom, which was, as I expected, stylishly messy, strewn with pretty trinkets, clothes, make-up and magazines. Its walls were mosaicked with photographs of her many friends on their many nights out and its low sloping ceilings were looped with lengths of sari fabric so you felt as if you were sitting in a circus top or perhaps a harem. Certainly it smelt like a harem – the air was thick with incense, which I suspect she mainly lit to disguise the stench of her cigarettes. During the first lesson I went out to the toilet and when I came back she had opened the dormer window and was lounging over the sill, cigarette in hand.

'*Tu en veux?*' She held out the pack of Marlboro Lights but I shook my head and took up *Villette* again. I knew she was expecting a reaction but I refused to rise to the bait. She blew the smoke out of the window and flicked the stub into the garden.

During the day I taught at a secondary school in Finsbury Park but I had started private tutoring in the evenings to save up for a deposit on a flat. Really, I disapproved of tutoring as my private pupils were already so privileged and enmeshed in a network of useful strings that they didn't deserve any more advantages. But, as I didn't have any parents to help with my deposit, as my only advantages were my brains and work ethic, and as I was determined to get out of my grim rented bedsit, I put my principles aside. Mr and Mrs Fenchurch had employed me to coach Jemima through her Oxford entrance exam. She was at the French Lycée in South Ken, which accounted for her habit of dropping into French, but apparently she wasn't getting the 'extra attention' she needed.

'She's a very sensitive girl,' Mrs Fenchurch had told me on the phone, before we met. 'People often don't realize how lacking in confidence she is and how much encouragement she needs.'

From the first lesson it was clear to me that Jemima was about as sensitive as a brick and no matter how much attention or encouragement she got, she was never going to pass the Oxford entrance. For a start she didn't even want to go to university, let alone Oxford.

'I'm so bored of studying,' she told me. 'Anyway Oxford will be full of boring geeks like Sarah.'

Sarah was Jemima's older sister, who was taking Classics at Christchurch. Photographs of her in the living room – there were none in Jemima's bedroom – revealed a smiley, wholesome girl with the same colouring as Jemima but without her allure. She certainly could not have got away with wearing a t-shirt with NERD on the front.

'What do you want to do instead of university?'

'Oh, I don't know. Nothing really… hang out with Alfie… have a good time.'

Alfie was Jemima's boyfriend. When she wasn't moaning about studying she was enthusing about him. From the photographs of him among her friends, I could see he was a spoilt-looking blonde boy with a face almost as pretty as Jemima's. He was three years older than her, had dropped out of university and now DJed and organized club nights around west London. His father was a banker.

'Surely you want a job though?' I said.

'God no.' Jemima laughed.

'But if you don't go to university, you'll have to work.'

'Why? What's so good about working?' Her tone, as always, was teasing.

'Well, it's just something that you have to do, to support yourself.'

'Mum and Dad support me at the moment and Alfie earns enough to support me in the future.'

'But you don't want to be dependent on Alfie.'

'Why not?'

'You'd get bored. It would be very unsatisfying. Work gives you a purpose.'

'My parents spend their whole time working and they're absolutely miserable.'

'They seem quite happy to me. Anyway, they're providing for you. To keep you in the style to which you've become accustomed.'

She giggled, as she did whenever I chided her. 'You're so harsh, Liza. Always putting me in my place.'

'That's my job.' I opened up *Villette*.

'Do you like your job?' she asked.

'Bits of it.'

'Which bits?'

'The bits where we talk about the books my pupils are meant to be studying.'

'What about getting to know your pupils? Do you like that?'

'Sometimes.'

'Am I your favourite pupil?' She shot me her most winning smile and I was struck once again by her prettiness. She had the kind of looks that ensured a head-start in obtaining happiness. In fact everything about her ensured a head-start in obtaining happiness.

'I don't have favourites. Come on, let's think about this essay question: "In what way might *Villette* be described as a feminist novel?"'

'Oh, God, I don't know. Remind me again, what is feminism?'

I glanced up from the closely-printed text clogged with my tight scribbles to Jemima's wide-smiled face. 'You don't know what feminism is? Jemima, feminism is one of the most important social movements of the last hundred years. If it wasn't for feminism, you wouldn't be here now getting an education, having all this –' I gestured with my Biro around the sweet-scented attic. '–all this freedom... You'd be married to Alfie already. You'd have to stay at home cooking and cleaning while Alfie –'

'–I was joking. Of course I know what feminism is. Equal rights and being all serious and having to go to work and never shaving your legs. To be honest I'd be quite happy being married to Alfie and staying at home cleaning.'

I surveyed her cluttered room and raised my eyebrows. 'I wouldn't say cleaning was one of your greatest talents. Anyway, think how constrained your life would be if you were never allowed to do your own thing, if you had to spend your whole life looking after Alfie, and you were entirely dependent on him for money…'

'I think it would be fine. Really pleasant actually.'

As the weeks passed and the exam loomed closer, Jemima grew less and less motivated. Her essays were all cut and pasted from the internet and less than half the word count I had asked for. She wasted time telling me about her nights out with Alfie or showing me presents he had bought her – Marc Jacobs perfume; a Vivienne Westwood ring; a set of Agent Provocateur underwear in cerise and black ('Don't tell Mum: she'd totally freak.') Questioning me about myself was another delaying tactic. I don't think she was particularly interested in the answers although sometimes her bright little eyes widened in amazement, or possibly pity, that someone could have had such a different and, in her view, horribly sad life compared to her: no, I didn't have a boyfriend; yes, I lived alone in Wood Green (an area she'd barely heard of let alone visited); no, I didn't grow up in London, I grew up with my godmother in Yorkshire (as off-the-map for Jemima as Wood Green); no, I never knew my parents: they died in a car crash when I was five.

I wondered whether to tell Mrs Fenchurch that Jemima was bound to fail. But usually she was still at work when I went round or, if she was there, she was on the phone or at her laptop. If she wasn't busy she looked too tired and irritable for me to pluck up the courage to bother her. Mr Fenchurch, on the other hand, was always so full of bonhomie that I didn't want to disappoint him with bad news.

The week before the entrance exam, I set Jemima an essay for homework: explain, with reference to relevant quotes, the ways in which Lucy Snowe is an unreliable narrator. When I turned up for her next lesson, she told me she'd been too busy to do it.

'Busy doing what?'

'I don't know. *Des trucs.*' She was lolling on her futon with a bag of Haribo sweets while I was upright at her desk.

'That's not a good enough excuse.'

'I had a really busy weekend. Alfie's going off to Spain for the winter. His friend's got him this residency DJing in Benicàssim. I'm not going to see him for four months and I really wanted to spend some time with him, so that's what I was doing all weekend.' She put a gummy bear in her mouth.

'Jemima, you're never going to pass if you don't make the effort.'

Sighing in an uncharacteristically sullen way, she examined her nails, which were painted bright yellow. 'I don't care,' she mumbled through a full mouth.

'You're an intelligent girl.' This wasn't true, of course, but I had to encourage her somehow. 'Don't you want to make something of yourself?'

She flicked her gaze up from under insolently heavy lids. 'What do you mean?'

'Well, use your brains. Be your own person. Not just be some sort of... appendage to some DJ.'

'"Appendage."' She laughed, but not in her usual jovial manner. 'Is that what you've done?'

'What?'

'Used your brains. Been your own person. Made something of yourself.'

'What?'

'If it wasn't for feminism you'd probably be married by now, have children, not have to be doing this boring job. God, if using your brains means ending up in your situation I'd rather not bother. I wouldn't want your life for a minute.'

Heat rose in my face as if she'd slapped it. I stood up. 'I'm going to go. We're obviously both wasting our time here.'

[57]

As I slipped down the four flights of stairs to the ground floor, I prayed I wouldn't bump into Mr or Mrs Fenchurch. Thankfully my prayers were answered.

The next two days I was on tenterhooks, expecting Mrs Fenchurch to ring and inform me my services were no longer needed. The Oxford entrance was on the Monday but I was set to continue teaching Jemima every Thursday until her A-levels the following summer. I wondered whether to ring Mrs Fenchurch first, explain that Jemima and I had fallen out. The explanations I rehearsed sounded schoolgirlish and ridiculous, like the kind of things Jemima herself would say. I wondered if I even wanted to carry on teaching her. Her words kept revolving around my head and, going through my usual weekend routines, I was struck by the dull, solitary smallness of my life. I could quite see that no one in their right mind would want it. As I perched on a folding chair in my tiny kitchen, waiting for the microwave to ping, while my individual portion of shepherd's pie revolved inside, I reflected that my default mode was to take up as little space as possible, whereas Jemima naturally lounged expansively and left her mark wherever she went. I wished I had more of a sense of entitlement, that I didn't always feel I had to apologize for existing, but I'd never been given as much as Jemima so I never felt I deserved as much. These thoughts had occurred to me before but I was usually able to push them out of my mind, squash out negativity with busyness. That weekend they were harder to shake. Two nights running I lay awake, feeling horribly alone, listening to the waves of traffic swishing in the distance. My bed was a flimsy raft and I was shipwrecked, swamped by the vast, harsh sea of London.

On Sunday, when I still hadn't heard from Mrs Fenchurch, I decided to email Jemima directly, ask if she still wanted me to come round on Thursday. My message was matter-of-fact. I did not refer to our altercation and wished her luck for Monday. By the time I went to bed that night, she had still not replied.

At quarter-to-eight the next morning my phone rang as I was preparing to leave for school. It was Mrs Fenchurch.

'I'm sorry to ring so early...' She sounded breathless and on the verge of tears. My thumping heart began to beat twice as fast. Before I could ask what was wrong, she told me they'd discovered Jemima's bed empty that morning with a note on the pillow saying she'd gone to Benicàssim with Alfie; that she was sick of studying and didn't want to do the Oxford entrance. 'It's the exam today. I can't believe it.' Her voice hardened. 'Did you know about this?'

'What?'

'That she didn't want to do the exam?'

'No, of course not.'

'But did you get a sense that things weren't right?'

'I... well... I think she was worried she wasn't going to pass.'

'And what did you think?'

'Well... she hadn't really done enough work and...' I wondered how honest I was allowed to be.

'... and?'

'... well, no. I don't think she would have passed.'

There was a long pause. 'Wasn't it your job to make sure she passed?' Mrs Fenchurch spoke with cold deliberation. 'Wasn't that what we were paying you for? Jemima is a very sensitive girl, very unconfident even though she puts up a very good front. She needed a huge amount of encouragement.'

I summoned up all my reserves of courage, which aren't great, and, in as cool and measured a tone as Mrs Fenchurch, I said, 'I can't work miracles. I tried my best but Jemima wasn't interested in studying.'

'It was your job to make her interested.'

'I tried my best.'

'That's your excuse: you tried your best?'

'Look, I'm sorry, Mrs Fenchurch, but I've got to go to work now, to my other job.'

'I don't think you tried hard enough.'

She cut me off before I could reply. Not that I would have had the guts to say what I really thought: be honest, Jemima was never going to get into Oxford. She's a good-time-girl, a child of pleasure. Work makes her listless and dejected. Parties and nightclubs are where she shines, where she can expand her butterfly wings and be the centre of attention; elsewhere, she droops and is dispirited.

I imagined Jemima would forget me but, strangely, she didn't. A few months later, I received an invitation from her to join Facebook. I'm a very private person and I'd resisted joining despite several invitations from others but curiosity about Jemima got the better of me. Trawling through her Facebook pages was like reading about an entirely different species of human being. I couldn't believe how many friends she had, how artlessly and ignorantly she commented on current affairs, how narcissistically she flaunted the happiness of her relationship with Alfie and how many pictures she had posted of herself, all of them highly flattering. Her status updates consisted of insights such as 'just drunk way too many margaritas! ;)', 'wearing my new pink bikini: feeling hot hot hot!!!;)' and 'is there anywhere you can get decent teabags in Benicàssim??!!' I gathered from these that she was still in Spain.

From time to time she sent me messages directly, which mainly consisted of bragging about what fun she was having. I replied with clipped interest but didn't offer much information about myself. I wondered what she got out of our one-sided correspondence and concluded that because I didn't admire her as readily as everyone else she came into contact with she valued my responses more.

Then, after a long silence, I, along with her 739 other Facebook friends, received an announcement that she had given birth to a baby boy. His name was Alfred after his father but he was to be known as Freddie. For the next few months I was treated to more boasting about little Freddie: how clever he was, how beautiful, how brilliant, how talented at smiling, burping, holding a rattle and sitting up unaided.

One day, I was coming out of Notting Hill tube on my way to another pupil's house – another lazy, pretty public schoolgirl called Zoë – when someone behind me said, in a familiar teasing tone, 'Well, if it isn't Liza Frost.'

There, behind me, was Jemima, in a tight pink dress, pushing a pram the size of a tank. Alfie ambled behind with his hands in his pockets.

'Hello, Jemima.' I kept all surprise out of my voice.

'It's so nice to see you. You look…' She looked me up and down, her smile never wavering. '… exactly the same.'

'And so do you.'

'I haven't put on any weight?' She twirled, displaying every side of her still slender figure.

'No, you look the same as ever.'

'Alfie, this is my old tutor, Liza. Liza, Alfie.' She ushered Alfie towards me, who shook my hand with complete indifference. 'I was such a pain, never did any work. You totally despaired of me, didn't you?'

I shrugged.

She turned to Alfie. 'Mum and Dad hired Liza to coach me through the Oxford entrance. And then I buggered off with you the day before the exam…' She squeezed Alfie's arm and he managed a non-committal smile. She turned back to me.

'… I'm so sorry, Liza. I was so annoying…'

I shook my head and gave a dismissive wave.

'… well, anyway, as you can see it all worked out fine in the end. As I knew it would… hey, don't you want to say hello to Freddie?'

I poked my head into the pram and self-consciously waggled my fingers at her little boy. Freddie responded with a gap-toothed, heart-melting grin and I had a sudden dismaying sense that, like his mother, he was destined for a wonderful life simply through the luck of inheriting beauty and money.

Jemima and I said our goodbyes, she promising to keep me updated on Freddie's progress, me promising nothing. I watched her sail queen-like up Notting Hill Gate, passersby parting either side of Freddie's enormous buggy, Alfie trailing in her wake. I had been wrong: she was nobody's appendage. I wondered why some people always got everything they wanted and others didn't, no matter how hard they tried or how worthy they were. I wondered why some people suffered and why some, like Jemima, suffered as little as any human being I have ever known

A Shower of Curates

Tania Hershman

Of late years an abundant shower of curates has fallen upon the north of England, all upon the land, and when they have earthed they stand, dust themselves off, slink away. Each has his own instructions, a map of sorts, and each has wiles and ways of translocating, spreading words and wishes. None will meet again and they feel no sorrow, not as ordinary folk might, you and I, had we been on such a journey. Have we been on such a journey? For my part, I think not. I measure my worth in these years by other means. The other day, in looking over my papers, I found in my desk the following copy of a letter, sent to me a year since by an old school acquaintance in which he bemoans – how strangely, how quite oddly! – the dearth of curates, the hollowness of temples in that time, and urges me – yes, me! – to think to join their ranks! If only I might share with him this news of the flood of them here now, of their filling of our holy – holy! – spaces, these so-called curates, these so called keepers of… Never matter now, I fear my time for medication is upon me. I have just returned from a visit to my landlord – the solitary neighbour that I shall be troubled with not much longer due to... well that must wait until another. That must wait.

Ah now, that is better, the draught has done its work, its holy work, yes! I am a one for that kind, I am that since – well, if you must know that you must go back with me to the autumn of 1827, stretch yourself to parse that far, that ancient year, before all that we now know, all that we grasp as essence, as import. My godmother lived in a handsome house in the clean and ancient town of Bretton and I, being summoned, and she not being one whose summons are ignored, found myself upon her path, thinking of that very school friend I have above alluded to. My godmother was spying from her window, she attempts to hinder me in so many ways, you would surmise she wished me gone forever. Not the kindly godmother my poor parents might have dreamed of, yet I am grateful for her challenges, they did thicken this skin of mine till today, although you might wonder at the medication I have already told of. That is another matter, purely chemical, I assure you.

'Child,' said she, although I was almost a man then. And we went into her parlour, and I saw in her eye that wickedness, and henceforth were we to become conspirators. And the result? Of course, you, being sharp of mind, already know, I need not spell out for you as if we were yet in nursery and you scream and I wail and the governess... I am distracted, tangents come and flow through me. I am amiss. Godmother and I, tis we two who brought about the surge in holy – holy! – men upon the land this day, she with her alchemy and I with my own, which came from what she taught to me but which I bent to my desires.

And what of these curates now? I feel them crawling to their places, I send out webs to each in turn, they are obedience personified, although not quite person, of course! They slink to their parishes, their teeth whiter than the whitest dentures you, my friend, will see, their smiles broad, their Biblical quotations sheer perfection.

'This,' said my godmother that day, 'will be our legacy, my child. Our life's work, this will be done...'

'Or undone!' I cried, for as I have mentioned I was not yet a man, but almost, and still given to outbursts. Godmother frowned and once again I was subject to her customary lecture: discretion, fewer words, secrets kept, mouths sealed shut. I blushed, lesson learnt.

I have yet varied the scheme a small amount and one curate fellow goes not to the holy place but my neighbour is even now unlocking his door to that broad smile, those Biblical quotations. It will not be long and then I shall purchase, for the matter of some small coins, the better land across that wall that I have long coveted. Godmother is not with me to see our success, or no longer corporeal, as she would have it, but she assured me she would watch from her celestial spot. Watch the foundations 'cross the land become as crumbs underfoot, the pinnings of society disease and flounder.

'Then to be reborn anew!' she said and for the one and only time, Godmother shewed her teeth, as pearls between those rosy lips.

Ah, I spy my neighbour now in conversation. Now it begins, now it is under way. I sit in my own parlour, comfortable, and I know, dear friend, that they will talk of this in decades hence, though they may never know from where it seeded, we have been so careful to obscure our part in this. Many will attempt to write on this, volumes will be filled, I have no doubt! And all true histories contain instruction; though, in some, the treasure may be hard to find, and when found, so trivial in quantity that the dry, shrivelled kernel scarcely compensates for the trouble of cracking the nut. But men being men will keep on and on. Men being men, are infinitely malleable, and were it not us, Godmother and I, it would have been some other. Our curates, they are abroad now, I sense it. Godspeed, my creatures. Godspeed, ha! Good night, my friend. Where now is my draught?

Behind all the Closed Doors

Sarah Dobbs

It was just like when they took Mutley in the middle of the night, thought Henry. Mutley was also a boy, but he would be the size of a pony and ponies couldn't live in houses with young boys. Mutley was an Irish Wolfhound pup. Henry thinks at least two of these words mean the same thing. Mutley has brillo-fur and granddad-eyes, despite being younger than Henry. He would lick Henry's hand like he always tasted good. The night they came to take Mutley, Henry had waited and waited. He had tried so hard to stare himself awake, like a Good Boy. He'd kept his arms round Mutley's neck, even when Mutley had wanted to get down and huffed and flopped his tail like those dead fish when Dad forgot to fill the pond back up.

Jenny is allowed to see. Jenny is Sensible and can do her gazillion times table. Jenny gets to go behind all the closed doors.

Sometimes Jenny catches Henry trying to peek through one of the doors. All he sees though are adults and feet. They laugh a lot, from deep inside their bellies. Henry wonders why nobody tells them to stop. Why nobody helps Dad, who shouldn't have to listen to people laughing.

'Henry!' Jenny hisses whenever her magpie-eyes pick him out.

'Jen,' Henry's dad will say and then Jenny will of course collect Henry and sit him on the bed and play The Beatles' *Twist and Shout*. Henry will set his face at her so she knows if she comes any closer, he'll scratch her face right off. She will shake her head at him like the adults do. Henry is never sure what they are saying no to.

Today, Henry thinks it is Monday. He feels for his specs and then lies staring at the ceiling. He turns onto his side and scratches at the Beatles sticker on his bedpost, listening to the house for clues. The sticker covers two initials he'd scratched into the post last month and was now embarrassed about: LN. Nobody has come to tell him to get his 'lazy bottom downstairs'.

Henry hauls himself up. His shoelaces creak as he manages to get the left shoe on and then attempts to repeat this success on the right one. The two tails shrug out. He starts again, smaller. Tighter. If only he'd been able to stay awake that time, Mutley would still be there. But even as he thought that, Henry knew it not to be true. They would have taken him another time. When adults want to do stuff, stuff happens.

Mutley has a new home now, they'd said. With old people who could take care of him better. How could old people, with their sticks and slowness be better than Henry? If Mutley had still been here, he'd bring him down to the kitchen where Henry would jingle his biscuits and last night's tea into the bowl. Henry would plod off late and Mutley would be wide-eyed and sneak an extra step towards him when Henry wasn't looking. This would mean Henry would have to be sensible: *No. Go home.* And Mutley's ears would go to sleep and his expression would be like he'd just farted.

'Henry, me lad!'

An adult he is related to ruffles Henry's hair, then palms his hand onto a creased shirt. He is in their kitchen. He smells of poo and pepper, Henry thinks. He has an accent which means he is from Dad's side, not Mum's. Henry scowls.

'Eggs,' this adult says. 'Perfect way to make 'em. Hard boiled, mash 'em up. Lashings a mayo, butter and pepper. Life's too short not to've butter, ay?'

Henry watches the adult frowning at him like he's forgotten something. He grips Henry's shoulder. When he's remembered what he'd forgotten, or is no longer bothered, the relative braves a smile. 'Want some?'

Henry curls his lip. 'Stinks that.'

The adult nods, shrugs, and Henry feels like he shouldn't be there because the man seems to need the kitchen all to himself.

Henry knows the route to school. He knows how the tips of his shoes look striding over cracks. *Break your mother's back.* Laces flapping from side to side like John Lennon's fringe flopping to *Twist and Shout*. He has 'the thing' wrapped in an Everton scarf he'd nicked after a match. It's stuffed deep into his satchel. No one this side of Stanley Park would touch it, not while wrapped in *The Toffees'* white and blue.

Henry skims stones at the rabbits on the traffic island, whizzing them like Dad had taught him on Tenby beach. They hold their paws to their chests and blink. His tummy hurts.

'Gyppo,' Henry tells Liz Naylor, who is eating her knuckles in assembly instead of saying the Lord's Prayer. 'When d'you last av a bath?'

She shrugs.

Henry folds his arms and plays with his laces. Remembers how his mum had clapped and told everybody when he'd first figured out how to do it. All by himself. He thinks of his satchel and what's inside, strung up on the pegs near the bogs.

In the mid-morning break, the milk-monitors come round. Henry thumbs the foil and downs his milk. Shows the girls his moustache. He blows a dull tune over the bottle and gets told to clear off. He circles the room then tasks himself with pulling out a strand of Liz's hair to see if he can do it without her noticing. She is drinking her milk at the time.

*

NURSE

Clutching his cheek, Henry is staring at the letters, white on black, trying to rearrange them. Make the U cover its head and grow a tail. The letters flex in his mind, change. Nance. That's the name Dad calls Mum. He checks again.

NURSE

A whiff of air, as if someone is blowing on him. He closes his eyes to feel it proper.

'Henry.'

People say his name a lot, but not much else. The nurse pats the chair and he dribbles into it slow, just so she knows she can't order him about. Comes at him with a pad. It stings.

'Bitch!'

Hands on her hips, she says, 'Henry.'

But she doesn't seem angry.

He is pretending he knows his six times table, scratching at the plaster the Nurse has stretched on his face. Too tight just to be a cow. Liz is staring right at him, chin high. Her mouth goes like this:

Six times six is thirty six, six times seven is...

He wants to punch Liz's nose and see if it springs back out again like a pillow. Instead he balls his fists and thinks he'll get her back by throwing stones at her like the rabbits on the way home. Henry mouths along, head down.

Eventually, the teacher wipes the board and writes $x7$. He can see the other numbers smeared but still there.

6

12

18

24

30

And he thinks, yeah, it's just like *that* too.

Henry watches his laces flip flop lazily. He doesn't want to get back to the house that doesn't have Mutley waiting, just to sit in his bedroom and listen to *Twist and Shout*. Not like anyone would notice if he never came home.

This park is not the one he's allowed to go to. It's the one where you'll 'get your 'ead kicked in Henry, lad.'

That'd show 'em.

He unwraps the scarf, spine curved and poking the bench. The book's cover makes Henry's tummy hurt worse. A dark, towering house is stamped on it surrounded by wide, empty sky. It's like how their house looks now. Opening the book he feels 'the thing' alongside, a dead weight, heavy through the scarf. He leaves it there and runs his finger along words that look like sewing, not like those in the rest of the book.

Dearest Jenny,

His finger squawks on the inside cover. Henry licks his lips, tongue catching on dead skin.

'Dearest,' he sniffs in the cold. *'Jenny.'*

Henry unwraps the other thing, struggles with the lever. The blade thrusts. He turns it around to look at the point then starts to scratch. The black ink greys, goes completely white in places. He tickles his little finger into the groove where the letters used to be. His finger can't quite touch the bottom of the indentation. Anger bottles up. He uses his nail to scratch a big H over the top. But Jenny's name still glares out in its half-whiteness.

Mouth tight, Henry starts to cut. Just a word at first: *solitary.* It itches on the page then gets properly lifted away by the wind. He watches it skid to a halt near the park railings, nesting with the litter. He'll look up what that means in the dictionary Mum gave him. When he gets home. His mood brightens; he has a purpose. He cuts another. Another one he doesn't understand: *mis-an-thro-pist's.* Henry's eyes narrow at the one next to the gap he has made. *Heaven.* He stares at that one and his eyeballs start to burn. In the ragged square where he'd sliced out *misanthropist's* another word has slotted into the gap. *Bitch.*

Henry frowns. He cuts out more words. Sentences. Whole pages.

vexatious phlegm
ill endure
inhospitable treatment
the first feathery flakes of a snow-shower

He doesn't know what all the words mean. They sound like how he imagines the old people who have Mutley would speak. He could look them all up. Paper flutters into the wind. Henry lifts his mouth and shows his teeth. Bye-bye. It's snowing words, he thinks.

His shoulders fall. And now he doesn't have anything to look up.

'There you are, Jesus!' It's the relative with the eggs. 'What the fu – you know, no. Think yer Dad hasn't enough on at the moment?'

Henry makes sure to walk two steps behind him the whole way back, to make the relative keep checking that he's there, which he does. Henry lets himself like the man a bit. He does look a bit like Dad. If Dad's features had been smudged away like the numbers on the board, like Mutley, in the middle of the night. He kicks the kerb. The relative frowns back at him. Henry gives him a black look. A bright pain rips through his toe. Tears swell; the wind tears them away.

Inside, the house is blue and cotton-wool-quiet. Sad blue. Henry remembers how it used to be mostly yellow. Dad is in the kitchen, looking like he's just woken up. His mouth opens and Henry holds his breath. Here it comes. He'll shout. So loud everyone'd hear.

'Found 'im.'

Doesn't even tell Dad which park. Useless, Henry thinks.

Dad nods and his eyes are narrowed in the same way Henry's do when he can't find his specs.

He sees their backs, the creak of feet, shoes on, up the stairs. He'd wanted to tell them about busting Liz's nose. He tears off the plaster and flicks it in the sink. There are no dishes at all but piles of food. His tummy mumbles like Mutley's would in the middle of the night. But the food all looks funny and smells of sick.

Henry unties his laces carefully and places the shoes by the door for brushing later. He is upstairs when he realizes nobody was going to do that.

Twist and Shout is already playing. His room smells of tickly perfume yuck: Jenny. He covers his ears and grits his teeth. Slams the door and waits to be told off. The needle zips, provides a beat of hopeful silence, then merrily starts back up again.

Jesus' naked body has fallen off the wall. Henry grabs Jesus and chucks him out the window. He pulls out the book from his satchel. Serves her right. The blade cores out pages, two at a time, sometimes three.

At first, he thinks it's something upended from his earlier tantrum. Wobbling to settle. He goes back to his work. *Crrrr* go the pages. There – again. Henry puts his knife down and throws the scarf over the book. Bits of the words she'd written to Jenny peep out from under the blue and white. Black little spider's legs.

He peers over at the cupboard. A mouse!

It's the fields, she'd told him. And you, lad. Messy little beggar dropping crumbs, eh? Her fingers on his lips brushing them like a guitar.

Gerrof, he'd said.

A smack on the bottom to push him off, to crouch and watch Dad set traps with milk-soaked bread, fag dripping out his mouth. Arse shining like the moon. Henry had stuck out his tongue and Mum had *thwapped* him with a tea towel. A memory of her baking potatoes warms his mood. Him and Jenny watching the oven for hours.

There it went again! Henry rises slowly, wincing at the *scree* of the bed springs. But the mouse has gone.

Henry growls, gets off the bed and goes to the cupboard. He sinks to his knees on the adjacent wall. It'll have gone down the back of the cupboard. If he sits still for long enough, the mouse might think he's a cupboard too.

He breathes as shallowly as possible.

The music stops. Pins and needles zorb up through his legs. The record player hisses, *bump, bump, bump*. Henry's thoughts scab with anger and his belly goes tight, thinking about them eggs he should've took this morning.

The mouse twitches.

He shouldn't look directly at it. His stomach goes *raaaaooooul*. The mouse freezes, then hitches forward. Big bugger! Its eyes are like them pins Mum would stick into Jenny's clothes when she was trimming them, to keep her place, she'd said. Pig-pink nose. He copies its twitching. Forgetting, he lifts his arm to wipe his own nose.

The mouse jerks. Gone. Henry has an idea. He gallops down the stairs, nearly colliding with Jenny who is coming out of a door that she remembers to close before he can see in. Not that he cares. He clatters through the cupboards, finds a heel of bread and dunks it in the remaining milk. Out the kitchen, he dashes back to put the bottle by the sink so it can be washed and returned.

'Henry.'

He rolls his eyes at his sister as he flies upstairs, shuts his own door and assumes the position; straight-backed near the cupboard. This time he keeps a hand on the floor, bread out on his palm. He has to wait so long he wants to eat it himself. Eventually, the mouse notches forward, careful, like when he's robbing penny sweets from the corner shop. It tries to take the bread. Misses. Comes back from another angle and has a nibble right there.

It has one foot on the pad of Henry's thumb. Tiny little scratch. Henry thinks about what it would be like to curl his fingers up. Ha! You're dead. To feel its body burst in his palms. Would it bleed? Would it be scared? Henry's mouth turns down and he starts to shudder. The mouse ditches him.

Some time later, blotchy-faced, Henry falls asleep, dizzy with tiredness. Since Mutley, he doesn't like to fall asleep. He expects to wake up and find that things have changed. The record player needle is still bumping, ensconced in the bubble of static it throws into the room, the weight of the darkness.

He dreams, or hopes to dream in those patches that are not definitely sleep or being awake, that the mouse will come back and sleep in his hand, unafraid.

At some point in the night (he will remember hearing it in the morning) there is a snipped metal squeak and a soft, fidgeting sound, like someone quickly searching through his sock drawer. His mind had urged him to get up, to help. Another part of him, the exhausted part, or the one that already knew, decided it wouldn't do any good anyway.

Before, someone would have come in during the night and righted the needle. Checked he'd had supper and brushed his teeth and put his 'jamas on. Either Mum, or someone she'd instructed to do it.

Henry woke in his school shorts and socks. One sock half off, droopy like an elephant's trunk.

'Where *is* it?!'

There's thumps next door, in the room he couldn't go in.

Jenny slams his bedroom door back.

'Come on, Jen, be sensible love.' A lady says this, someone with the shape of his mother's face, but not hers. More swollen, especially today. Her name is Lucy or Lynne. Other adults stand, shadowy, behind her. Clouds of people. Whispering like trees in autumn. Lucy or Lynne usually brought currant loaf.

Henry looks at her hands, frothing with tissue.

Jenny stamps her foot. 'What have you done?'

He scratches his cut from Liz. His chin shrinks back.

His sister, being Sensible, the one they entrusted the house key to when they were going to be late, is screaming like one of those cars people brought for Dad to mend. Screaming in their quiet house. The rag and bone cart clops over the cobbles outside, the man bellowing something unrecognisable and deep and Henry realizes he's late. Why'd nobody woken him up?

'Be late for school.' He struggles to right his sock.

'Henry. Love,' the lady who looks like Mum but not, says.

'I know he's got it.'

Jenny strides past him and wrenches aside his bed covers. Henry tries to get up off the floor but his legs are dead. 'Argh! Ai.' He hops, one foot spinning with pins and needles.

He sees her, they all do, gripping something blue and white. Rags it off the bed. The blade twirls and flashes. Adults draw in their breaths. Something heavy thuds onto Henry's tea-coloured carpet, words flailing out of tattered pages.

Jenny wails so hard Henry wraps his arms around himself. Dad looks from one to the other. Jenny is hunched over the book, has it gathered to her belly. Henry watches her fingers stroke the inside cover, as his had done.

'It was her… favourite, I –'

'Yeah, to you!'

Jenny screws up her face in question, first at Henry, then at the wall of adults. Henry looks to Dad to intervene but he seems slack.

Something glints and Henry notices the trap beyond Jenny's feet, under the bed. Holding tightly to something white and soft and still. As if it will never let it go.

'Why, Henry? It was her favourite.'

Henry starts at that – *It was her favourite*. A pulse of shock. The realisation of something he half-knows already. Something has changed in the night.

The adults seem to feel embarrassed and thin out, circling at a distance. The front door goes; movement, voices. Outside-people who don't know they don't talk that loudly in here anymore.

The record player needle still goes *thunk, thunk*.

A ragged cloud of paper with a whirl of letters lands on Henry like some moth. 'Wu-Wuth…'

Jenny sighs. 'What you on about?'

He chews his mouth to one side. 'So wossit mean, eh?'

Jenny closes the book. Shrugs. 'Turbulent.' At his expression, she says, 'Like really bad wind.'

'Like Mutley.'

Jenny looks like she likes him again, Henry thinks.

'Why's it her favourite?'

His sister's thumb strokes the book's empty sky. 'Hero was from round here, she said.'

'So what?'

She shrugs. 'Reminded her of you or something, I dunno. Turbulent.'

'Don't smell,' he says. But really, he thinks Jenny's probably said something really nice.

'Ugh! Fine. I don't know.' Jenny raises her eyebrows, gets up. He thinks she's just going to leave, leave him with the

[77]

awful blankness of the thing he's realized, but she picks up the needle and rests it back on its cradle. 'I'll read it to you someday.'

'Hate that song.'

'Thought it was your favourite.'

'Not now.'

Henry blinks. 'I wanted to see her too.'

Jenny looks at him, eyebrows crumpled with how much she hurts. They soften. 'But she's...' She glances to the door, listening. 'It was the middle of the night Henry and we thought... we...'

Henry's sister watches him and then takes his hand, pulls him over the landing, and opens a door.

Sometime, in the next few days, he isn't sure when he notices or when it happens, when he even thinks to check, but someone has taken the mouse, and the trap, away.

Chapter XXXVIII – Conclusion (and a little bit of added cookery)
with abject apologies to Charlotte Brontë

Vanessa Gebbie

Reader, I did not marry him.

Oh, it would have been an interesting enough wedding, quiet of course, no guests save the bride, the groom, the parson, the clerk. And I dare say, when we got back from church, I might have gone into the kitchen, where Mary would have been cooking the dinner, John cleaning the knives, and I might have said –

'Mary, there's a thing. I seem to have married Mr Rochester this morning!' But I did not. Mary therefore had no cause to look up and stare at me: and the ladle with which she was basting a pair of roasting chickens had no cause to hang suspended in air for a minute or so. Nor did John's knives take a similar rest from the polishing process.

I did however enter the kitchen, unwed, on my way to fetch a vase for the daffodils. I did listen unwillingly to a basting Mary who mumbled:

'I seed you go out with the master, I thought you was gone

to church to be wed...' And John, when I turned to him, was grinning from ear to ear.

'Nah,' he said, sucking his tooth. 'I telled Mary how it would be. I knew you wouldna do it, Miss!' and he politely pulled his forelock. Why do men *do* that? It is most mystifying. I did not react instantly, however, just smiled that slight smile for which I am known, and said, 'Thank you, John. I am gratified indeed.' I searched about in my tippety-pocket. 'Mr Rochester told me to give you and Mary this...' I put into his hand a notice of impending redundancy. Dear Mr Rochester had finally enrolled at a cookery school and would have no further need of Mary's concoctions.

Without waiting to hear more, I left the kitchen. In passing the door of that sanctum some time after, I saw Mary and John still poring over the paperwork, and I caught the words –

'You worked un oat, yet, Mary? Bugger me and I wish I'd larned to read and noat juss mouth in this unfathomable accent what do not transfer willingly-like to t'page.'

I wrote to Moor House and to Cambridge immediately, for I was withholding something vital, reader, for the conclusion. Diana misread my letter, however, construing that I was now a married woman. She announced that she would just give me time to get over the honeymoon, and then she would come and see me.

'Get over the honeymoon?' said I to Mr Rochester, 'Why, what does she think we might have got up to had we wed, which we have not, but had we – oh I am only a simple girl!' but then I pondered this last, adding, 'But an intelligent one, that must not be forgotten...' and another addition, 'rather perspicacious...' and yet another... 'and above all, modest...'

I read her letter to Mr Rochester, as his latest cookery magazines, which he had been so looking forward to, had not arrived – it being so far out here, for the poor postman.

'I cannot think,' he cried, similarly nonplussed. 'Blanche

Ingram always said I had a lot to learn.' He shook his head, and waved a recipe for stuffed quail at the wall. 'I thought she meant I could improve my French.'

Dear Mr Rochester. At some point we will have to read up on all this, but for now I was glad to lend an ear to his bewailings.

'Oh, Jane...' he seemed lost in reverie. Then he looked up, his face a mask of incomprehension. 'And Bertha too, such a fiery temperament. I am told my lack of skill in the rumpy pumpy department contributed to her indisposition... she went quite mad in the end.'

'Telling me,' I said. 'The curtains on the spare room bed have never recovered. Nor has Thornfield Hall, come to that.'

He hung his head. 'Oh, I tried. But they never came out of the oven right...'

'What didn't, light of mine eyes?' I enquired.

'Rumpies,' he said. 'My very own interpretation of the rum baba recipe handed down by my great grandmother. Rochester Rumpies.'

I sighed. 'Something tells me we all have a lot to learn.'

He returned to our latest missive from Diana. 'She does not mention her brother. How is he? Does he write to you?'

I told him – how St John received any news, I don't know, as he never said when he wrote, just sent a copy of his latest sermon. Indeed, St John has maintained a regular, though not frequent, correspondence ever since: he hopes I am happy, and trusts I am not of those who only mind earthly things. I advised him to drop the affected 'St' from his name, and be content to be simply 'John'. I wrote thusly: 'It is quite possible that your good lord would not approve of those who canonize themselves before their demise.' He did write back immediately, arguing his case most eloquently, and it was not until I pointed out that a man called John was fairly important in the Bible, did he relax and concur.

You have not quite forgotten little Adèle, have you, reader?

I do try, for she is such a pain, but I cannot; I soon asked and obtained leave of Mr Rochester to go and see her at the school where he had placed her. Her frantic joy at beholding me again moved me to leave her there for a further year or two, for she had not changed. She looked pale and thin: she said she was not happy, she talked non-stop, mostly about herself. However, I relented. I found the rules of the establishment were too strict, its course of study too severe for a child of her age, and anyway, a girl-person, what would such learning do but place her outside the norm? One ought not be beautiful, rich and well-educated. Education belongs to the plain of face, like moi. See, je can speak le Français.

I took her home with me. I meant to become her governess once more, but I soon found this impracticable; my time and cares were now required by another – my plans were bearing fruit. So I sought out a school conducted on a more indulgent system, and near enough to permit of my visiting her once a term, and bringing her home sometimes, in the holidays. I took care she should never want for anything that could contribute to her comfort: Mr Rochester made a habit of baking a different cake each week, and it was despatched to Adèle by phaeton. She soon settled in her new abode, became very happy there, and made fair progress in her studies, but sadly, if unsurprisingly, she still had no friends.

As she grew up, a sound English education corrected in a great measure her French defects; where once she had been non pc, over-excitable, bolshy and lacking any sort of moral compass, when she left school, I found in her a pleasing and obliging companion: docile, good-tempered, and well-principled. By her grateful attention to me and mine, she has long since well repaid any little kindness I ever had in my power to offer her.

My tale draws to its close, reader: one word respecting my experience of married life, and one brief glance at the fortunes of

those whose names have most frequently recurred in this narra-
tive, and I have done, and will repair to the withdrawing room to
partake of a small glass of raspberry cordial with my beloved.

Mr Rochester continued cooking until his concoctions were
the talk of society. Oh, yes, he was completely blind for the
first two years, and, occasionally, mistook ingredients, with the
most amusing results. His sardine and raspberry soufflés, sent
to Blanche Ingram's for her wedding, caused mayhem, but then
she always needed a rocket up her bustle, don't you think?

It was one afternoon in the downstairs pantry when I realized his blindness was lifting. Until that moment, I had been
his vision, and, had naught changed, I would still be stuck at
his right hand. Literally, I was (what he often called me) the
apple of his eye. But oh, it was such a pother. He saw books
through me; and oh how I did weary of gazing for his behalf,
and of putting into words the effect of field, tree, town, river,
cloud, sunbeam – of the landscape before us; of the weather
round us – and impressing by sound on his ear what light
could no longer stamp on his eye. The only fun to be had
was in invention – I would turn on the faucets in the laundry
room, have him stand by an open window, and declare us to
be transported to the very top of the highest waterfall in the
district. 'You durst not move, my dear Mr R,' I would declare.
'Stay still. I will return by nightfall...' and I would withdraw
for the rest of the day to indulge in more pleasant pastimes.

Oh how did I weary of reading to him; how did I weary
of conducting him where he wished to go: of doing for him
what he wished to be done. Was this the only reason why I
was on this earth? He claimed these services without painful
shame or damping humiliation. He loved me so truly, that
he knew no reluctance in profiting by my attendance: he felt
I loved him so fondly, that to yield that attendance was to
indulge my sweetest wishes. But oh, dear reader, how wrong,
how very wrong he was.

One morning at the end of the two years, as I was writing a letter to his dictation, filling it with deliberate spelling mistakes, he came and bent over me, and said —'Jane, have you a glittering ornament round your neck?'

I had a gold watch-chain: but petulantly, I answered, 'No.'

'And have you a pale blue dress on?'

I had, but said it was yellow. He informed me then, that for some time he had fancied the obscurity clouding one eye was becoming less dense; and that now he was sure of it.

He and I went up to London. He had the advice of an eminent oculist; and he eventually recovered the sight of that one eye. He cannot now see very distinctly, but enough to no longer make marmalade and basil soup or serve roast Pomeranian for dessert with crème Anglaise... he cannot read or write much; but he can find his way through a simple recipe for dropped scones without being led by the hand.

My Mr R and I, then, are happy of a sort: and the more so, because those we most love are happy likewise. Mary Rivers married: once every year, she and her husband, Mr Wharton, come to see us, and we go to see them. Mr Wharton is a clergyman, a college friend of her brother's, and, from his attainments and principles, worthy of the connection, although he cheats at rummy and bathes only once a quarter. We plan our visits carefully.

As to St John Rivers, he left England: he went to India. St John is unmarried: he never will marry now. (Who would marry him, reader? Look at the verbiage up with which one would have to put.) Himself says he has hitherto sufficed to the toil, and the toil draws near its close: his glorious sun hastens to its setting. I am told this means his life nears its end, although why on earth we do not use simple language and resort instead to euphemism beats me.

We are all most relieved to be settled, finally. The last letter I received from St John drew from my eyes human tears, (as opposed to crocodile, perhaps?) and yet filled my heart with divine joy: he anticipated his sure reward, his incorruptible crown. Typical. Each to his own, I say. Crowns have never sat well on me – one's hair, caught back in a simple but tasteful bun, would never suit.

And now, mine own conclusion. Dear reader, I was promised a visit from Diana Rivers, you will recall. And she came, pretending joy at my supposed marriage to Mr R. Her proximity and my bounding heart would not allow the maintenance of deceit – in no time at all our love for each other was declared, and we now live together in companionable and consummate bliss. We have to put up with Mr Rochester in a ménage à trois, and his obsession with truffle-hunting for his *espárragos con trufas* is hard to bear. But that is a small price to pay for true happiness.

The end.

That Turbulent Stillness

Elizabeth Baines

The trouble was – I can tell you – she was prone to taking her cues from Brontë heroines.

I know very well what happened. When she caught sight of Kevin Flanagan in his black bomber, sauntering along the towpath towards her and Pam, a hole was punched in the bright suburban day, and also in her heart. That's how it felt.

They were just by the cemetery. On the left, from between the tall trees and the looming mausoleums, came a ferny scent of death like a challenge. On the right, the water gelled as if changing chemical composition.

Ahead, Kevin Flanagan's white cigarette arced.

Everyone at school had told them: the Flanagans were tinkers, or had been, before Kevin Flanagan's father fetched up one day in this north-Midlands market town and something about its calm grey square and its church like a frosted cathedral basking in a hollow – or maybe debt, or a feud, who knows? – prompted him to stop moving and settle. He still plied his trade, selling something, nuts and bolts perhaps, his old caravan parked up as an office in the family's back yard in the part of town where tiny brick terraces ran down narrow cobbled streets. Kevin Flanagan was the eldest of several children.

He wasn't tall; he was stocky but slim, powerful-looking, with strong features that scowled from under a forelock of reddish-brown hair. She'd seen him once or twice with other lads on a street corner when she and Pam had juddered on their bikes down the cobbles, and once at the back of the cinema queue. Each time, in spite of her private school, her parents with their company cars and the big detached home on the wide North Road, she recognized Kevin Flanagan as a fellow spirit.

He reached them on the towpath. He broke from his frown into a grin, his eye tooth gleaming, and the hole in her chest punched wider.

They got talking. He leaned on the cemetery wall, one foot up behind him.

The trouble was, it was Pam he seemed to want to talk to, Pam who didn't wear glasses and whose mini-skirts were shorter; it was Pam he offered a drag on his fag.

She watched Pam taking it, her little finger crooked. A silence had fallen and she was aware of Kevin Flanagan staring at Pam too as she inhaled dramatically, eyes closed, lids flickering and sheeny.

Nearby, on the railway bridge over the canal, the rails began to hum: beyond the edge of the town the Flying Scotsman was approaching.

Kevin Flanagan broke the spell. 'Come on! Let's get under the girders!'

It's what the local lads did: swing themselves up to lie in a narrow gap at the top of the concrete pillar supporting the bridge, inches from the monster pounding above.

'You're joking!' said Pam, but *she* said, 'OK!' and they were running, the two of them, her and Kevin Flanagan, they were under the bridge – the rails were ringing now, you could hear the engine thundering – and he was levering himself up, big thighs flexing, then reaching down from his horizontal position to hand her up after him, and just as the engine exploded onto the bridge, his huge hands clamped her to his side.

And the train detonated over them, juddering the girders, vibrating the concrete, thundering through her organs, her blood, filling her ears with a noise so loud it swelled to a kind of silence. On and on – all twelve or so carriages – and there in the whirlwind of noise and vibration she became aware of his body beside her, the swell of his thigh against her own, his big spatulate hands lying now on his hard flat belly, his exotic sharp-musty smell. And in that clamouring silence, in that turbulent stillness, all the middle-class caution of home and school was pounded away.

The last carriage left the bridge, the noise snapped off like a shutter; real silence floated in. They leaned up on their elbows, embarrassed now to be so close to each other's bodies, and she began to lever herself down.

Her body felt weightless.

Pam, waiting down below in her pastel clothes, looked domestic, like a puppet, and she knew in that moment that she wouldn't be going around with her much anymore.

Just before she jumped, he swung his legs to follow down behind her and his knees caught her shoulders.

She thought of him as her Heathcliff, of course.

Her father hated him, as he was bound to.

In what dubious dealings was Kevin Flanagan's father involved? he wanted to know. Where had he come from? Why did nobody know?

She rolled her skirt higher at the waist, she checked on her bird's nest hairstyle and left her father with questions dropping round him unanswered, unanswerable, like crumpled false starts on paper.

Even Kevin, who'd been a baby when they settled here,

didn't know the answers. Not that she asked him. What she loved was precisely the not knowing, the history wiped, she and Kevin new-born into a brand-new story in which he was the only hero and she the only heroine.

He started work at the paper mill. He bought a motorbike second-hand from a friend and, against her father's strict injunction, she hopped on the back. He kicked the starter, his eye tooth gleaming, and they roared away from the placid square, the closed shops with their lowered eyes, the church encrusted with history, sending up dry suburban leaves in whorls, making for the moors at the top of the Pennines, for the scouring heather and the wide possibilities of empty sky.

Though as they sat in the heather he'd stare away at the undulating surface, his face half-hidden beneath his tawny forelock, his full lips drawn down at the corners. He was broody and silent, but then he never talked much anyway, and though in these moments she was disappointed by his distance she loved his inchoate passion, so like her own.

She left school. She left the home of her despairing parents to live with Kevin Flanagan in a one-room flat above the Co-op in the market square, approached from the alleyway behind. She got a job in the gift shop. She laughed at her parents' protestations that if she wanted to be free and avoid a life of small-town bourgeois values, then selling overpriced tat for a minimum wage was hardly the way. They missed the point: that if you lived a life of passion, then working in a gift shop hardly defined you; that if you lived a life of passion nothing else mattered.

She had brought her books, her shelf of novels, but what mattered was *life*: those moments when, back from work first, she'd look out at the square and see Kevin weaving his motorbike across it towards her, when moments later his key turned in the lock and there was his leather-clad form, silhouetted in a blare of afternoon sun.

Of course, because of their passionate natures they quarrelled – about nothing, things she couldn't afterwards remember, or because when he came home late she felt jealous of the time he'd spent with his mates and with strangers, in garages or pubs, wheeling and dealing. But as they yelled at each other over the room, as he threw down his keys in exasperation, the athletic curve from his straight shoulder to his large loose hand, the tight flex of his leather thighs, the whole air he'd brought back of other worlds out there waiting, would all break her resolve, and she'd rush to him, and he would melt too, his wired limbs becoming fluid, and they'd fall into bed, fusing together. *I am Kevin*, she would think, *and he is me.*

It was ridiculous that she should feel jealous. He was doing it for her, for their future together. He had so many plans. Already he had a foot in several businesses. He was working now for a building firm and there was talk of his being taken into the partnership; along with the partners he had a share in a Sheffield nightclub. The idea of a pizza takeaway – and in the future a nationwide chain – was in the air.

All her parents' predictions were proving wrong.

'We're going places, you and I,' he told her, pushing her back on the pillows, his torso silky in the lamplight. Outside in the square the town hall clock struck the hour, and she thought of the sound pooling over the town, rippling in circles out over the villages and on to the dark wild hills.

She was buying tomatoes in the market one Saturday when someone said her name. She looked up and there beside her was Trevor Sugden. In the private school, Trevor Sugden had fancied her – no, he'd been *sweet on her*, that was the more appropriate old-fashioned phrase. He was an old-fashioned boy, who would stare at her intently through his horn-rimmed glasses, his pupils brimming with admiration, or love, or whatever it was she didn't like to think of him feeling for her. He had made her squirm.

He'd been away at university, and she hadn't seen him now

for about two years.

She stared. It had to be said that he looked more present-able now: his jeans had a tighter, trendier cut, and his wind-cheater jacket was at least half decent. There were the eyes, still brimming but steadier now, enough for her not to cut him dead but to say, 'Hey, Trev, how y'doin'?'

Calling him *Trev*, of course, was cruel. It sounded sarcastic, he was definitely a *Trevor*, never a *Trev*. And sarcastic was how she felt, or rather, no, something more subtle – a kind of pity-ing thrill at her own escape from everything he stood for. She wanted to prolong the sensation; she said, 'I'm going for a coffee. D'you want to join me?'

He followed her between the market stalls to the café – he didn't shuffle or drag obsequiously behind as she might have expected, but she could feel him respectfully letting her lead the way.

They sat in the window.

She told him straight away where she was living, and that she was living with a boyfriend, pointing over the market awn-ings to the window of the flat and its secretively gleaming panes. As he glanced at it and nodded, she saw how deliber-ately he kept a bland expression on his face, and she did then feel compunction. He told her about his studies, and the city he was studying in. She was a little surprised by the quietly confident air with which he spoke about it all, and by the way, when the waiter brought him the wrong coffee, he got the matter put right, cheerful and matter-of-fact. He was home for the Easter holidays, he told her, helping his father who ran the furniture business settle into new premises in the town. A prime site it was, he said, just off the market square.

He was clearly ready to tell her all about it. She looked away, impatient.

He said, intent and apparently oblivious to the fact that he was being discouraged, 'It wasn't easy securing it. There were others interested.'

She looked out of the window.

'In the end it all came down to a vote on the council. And really, if it hadn't been for Councillor Irwin…'

She thought, trust Trevor Sugden to go to university and end up entangled in small-town politics. She stopped him right there.

She stood up. She hadn't even finished her coffee.

She said, 'I have to get back. Kevin will be getting home.'

'Kevin?'

'Yes, Kevin Flanagan. You know him…'

Of course, everyone knew Kevin Flanagan. She watched Trevor's eyes widen, his cheeks colour. Of course, wild, romantic handsome Kevin Flanagan, against whom no nerdy ex-grammar-school boy would ever stand a chance.

Kevin was hunched at the table as she entered.

Something was wrong.

His fists were clenched.

She put the tomatoes on the table and they lay before him, greasily pregnant in their plastic. 'What's the matter?'

He'd been home a while. He said, 'I saw you from the window, going into the café with that bastard!'

She laughed. The word was so inappropriate for someone quite so ineffectual as Trevor Sugden, but also she was shocked that Kevin should have so little faith her, so little faith in himself, shocked at the very idea, so alien to what they had between them, that she'd be tempted by anyone else at all, leave alone Trevor Sugden. But also she was touched by the strength of his passion.

She put her hands on his clenched shoulders. She turned him towards her, laughing at the ridiculousness of his assumption, and felt him relax.

She thought she had reassured him.

Two days later the police came.

The previous evening, along with a mate, he had sought out Trevor Sugden who was stacking boxes alone in his father's new premises, and they'd given him a beating that had put him in the hospital on a life support machine.

She lay awake that night, images blossoming like bruises: his head bowed, as they charged him, the droop of his forelock; his leather back view as they led him away. The images she tried to squeeze away: bandages and harsh hospital lights, the bleeping of medical machines...

The night felt hollow, a deep crevasse into which their passion had fallen and was rolling, bloodied with violence.

'Come home,' her mother said on the phone.

She was at the window. The midweek traders were packing up their stalls. Boxes lay around, flattened cardboard was stacked in piles for the binmen, paper flapped around the feet of the scaffolds.

She thought, yes, she might go.

She remembered his head cocked away as they charged him, as if he didn't want to face what he'd done, his shoulders held straight as they led him down the stairs, as if in a bid to withstand himself.

The way that, out of shame, he didn't meet her eye.

Outside, a piece of paper unlocked itself from a metal pole, skidded over the flagstones and became airborne, rising high above the awnings, and up to the roofs and over, towards the prison.

She thought of him in his cell. She saw him lift his head, the forelock sliding. She imagined him mouthing her name.

It was as if, like Jane Eyre, she heard him calling, her lover lost in the darkness of his passion.

'No,' she said to her mother, 'I won't come home.'

Though she couldn't, in all conscience, ignore Trevor Sugden.

Daffodils shivered on the hospital lawn; her feet made icy

crushing on the gravel drive.

As she entered his room, Trevor Sugden was easing himself gingerly onto his bed. Plaster and wadding covered his nose. Three weeks after the attack, the bruises on his face were circled with yellow.

He didn't speak. He gestured to the chair.

She said, 'Trevor, I'm so sorry.'

His voice was nasal and thick through the dressings. 'It isn't your fault.' He sighed. 'To some extent I have myself to blame.'

She said, 'No –' but he went on.

'I should have locked the door. It's not as if we hadn't been warned. We got the council vote, but those pizza takeaway guys, they weren't going to give up. They'd broken the window already. They were out to frighten us off.'

She gasped, 'No...! That's not why Kevin... Trevor, you've got it wrong!'

Over the ridiculous dressing, he was looking at her steadily. 'He warned me himself. He came up to the old premises the day before we moved.'

He sighed. 'I could kind of see his point. He said: "You middle-class bastards with your friends on the council." And he gave me a pretty clear warning; he said: "You and your fucking father won't be getting in my way, mate."'

The word – *mate* – came out like a cough, and Trevor winced over his broken ribs.

So, reader, she didn't marry Kevin Flanagan. She. I. I didn't marry him. Now, these years later, I see her, my former self, as another person, the heroine, like Cathy, only of a story within a story. And like Cathy's housekeeper Nelly Dean, I watch her from out of a bigger, wider story, and sigh and smile...

My Dear Miss...

Zoë King

My dear Miss Woodhouse,

Pray forgive this intrusion. I am Miss Jane Eyre, late of Thornfield Hall of North Yorkshire where I imagined I had found a home until circumstances proved otherwise. Your name has been given to me as one who is wise in matters of the heart.

I find myself in something of a quandary. I had been engaged to marry one Edward Fairfax Rochester, to whom I had a deep and growing attachment, despite his being described as 'queer, ugly and cynical'. Perhaps I should have been wiser. Perhaps I should have listened to those who warned me of his singularly cavalier regard for the institution of marriage.

I will own, Mr Rochester has not the eloquence nor the gentility of the gentlemen who frequent your social circle. However, despite my standing in his employ, he has only ever treated me as an intellectual equal.

The truth, Miss Woodhouse, is that despite the many obstacles between us, I came to know a growing passion for him, only for it to be dashed in light of the revelation that he already housed a wife, and this revealed only moments before our marriage.

Of course I had to flee. And now, via a circuitous route through which I shall not weary you, I find myself in the care of one Mr St John Rivers, a devout and earnest man of the cloth, who proposes that I should join him as his wife, while he travels as a missionary to the Indian continent. However, despite his many qualities, I cannot but see him as a 'professional Christian', a cerebral man, devoid of passion, of heart, and yet not devoid of a controlling nature, a man who would bend me to his will, while my own passions must be buried, eventually to wither.

I hope, I think, Miss Woodhouse, you will understand my concern. Life has thrown up these two opposing prospects for my future. If I am to be subjugated to a man, must it be via either of these two routes? Is there not an alternative? Please advise with all due haste as Mr Rivers is pressing me for a decision.

Yours most sincerely,
Jane Eyre

My dear Miss Eyre,

How I understand your dilemma. Mr Rochester has been described to me as being entirely without charm, despite his apparent wealth. Obviously he is your social and economic superior, yet his recent behaviour behoves one to feel he is almost entirely without manners.

By any and all accounts, Mr Rivers is a man of singular vision. He is intent upon 'doing good', but alas, it appears that good is about his own particular brand of Christianity. His is not a compassionate ministry; rather it seems it is about a quest for personal glory, to the detriment of those around him. Is he seeking a wife, or an instrument to assist him in his quest, a helpmeet, if you will?

Miss Eyre, I beseech you, allow me to introduce you to some of my own circle of friends, friends I have come to value and admire, for their eloquence, their social stature, their prudence, and their equanimity, qualities which neither Mr Rochester nor Mr Rivers can by any means lay claim to.

Of course, I appreciate that we are not social cousins, and yet, I so admire your perspicacity in claiming a life for yourself, regardless of the murmurings of those who would hold you beneath them. A woman such as yourself, with both the intellectual means and the determination to go forward in life, must surely deserve a wider and more genteel following. Indeed, I have this very evening discussed possibilities with my dear friend, Mr George Knightley, who of course cautions me against such endeavours, and yet I cannot eschew such a mission.

May I, Miss Eyre, prevail upon you to join us in Highbury for a time? We have here a certain young clergyman, Mr Elton, a handsome and intelligent addition to our circle. My thought was to bring him to my dear protégé Harriet Smith but, alas, he has entirely misread my interest in him. Poor silly Harriet imagined herself in love with a local farmer but I have persuaded her to reject his suit as I am convinced she should marry a gentleman. Of course a pretty man may choose his own wife, but one would wish Mr Elton would be more circumspect in his dealings. Poor Harriet has developed feelings for him but his attentions have been directed elsewhere, with rather disastrous results.

Please tell me you will accede to my request, which is offered with all generosity. Your presence here would be of decided benefit to myself, to poor Harriet and also to Mr Elton, who would no doubt prove a ready friend in your time of need.

I am, yours most affectionately,
Emma Woodhouse

Dear Miss Woodhouse,

Thank you for your letter of 14th inst. Alas, you appear to have misunderstood my dilemma. Mr Rochester is not without charm, though it is not the easy charm with which you appear to be acquainted. My separation from him has nothing to do with lack of regard, and everything to do with Christian propriety. He is a married man, albeit the marriage is hollow. However, my connection with him is born of deeper concerns than mere frippery, though you appear to demonstrate little understanding of such things.

Having carefully considered Mr Rivers' offer, I have indicated to him that I cannot accept. Thanks to a recent inheritance I am not without means, so I have suggested to him that I will accompany him as his sister. My dear cousin Diana has urged me to eschew any ideas of marriage to her brother, but my refusal has upset Mr Rivers to the extent that he now feels I have placed myself beyond the bounds of true Christianity. It is, he feels, my *duty* to accompany him as his wife!

As regards Mr Elton, of course I regret that Miss Smith has been so cruelly treated but quite why you imagine I might be of help is entirely beyond me. You speak as though you expect me to take Mr Elton 'off your hands', or to bring him around to your way of thinking, but as you say, a pretty man may choose his own wife. Clearly Mr Elton has a mind of his own, and will indeed do so, regardless of your meddling.

Forgive my sharpness, Miss Woodhouse; life appears to me to be too short to be spent in nursing animosity. I would ask you to trust however that when I light upon my second-self, I will know it. Despite my initial approach to you, I now find I need no intermediary; my decisions are my own.

Yours sincerely,
Jane Eyre

My dear Miss Eyre,

Despite your entreaties, I find myself unable to set aside your dilemma. Your situation as it regards Mr Rochester is impossible, as you yourself have owned. I would implore you however to look elsewhere for a solution to the question of your future.

I have no doubt life as a missionary has its compensations, but I cannot believe it would feed the passion of a soul such as yours. I hope and trust that by the time you read these words a solution will have presented itself which does not involve you travelling to India with a man who has but little regard for your future happiness.

As ever, yours very affectionately,
Emma Woodhouse

My dear Miss Woodhouse,

With regard to my last, I regret my sharpness of tongue and would ask for your forgiveness. I found myself deeply troubled, not least by the notion that my clarity of thinking had been sacrificed to the pressure being put upon me by my cousin, Mr St John. However, I now find I am almost of the mind to accept his entreaties, as he appears to be entirely sincere in his fears for my soul.

I shall ask the heavens for guidance.

Yours most sincerely,
Jane Eyre

My dear Miss Eyre,

Would that distance did not separate us so! I implore you to reconsider this decision. It is my considered opinion that a life of single piety would bring you more solace than a life spent sharing the cold aims of a man who sees you only as a means to an end, and that end his own soul's redemption!

Please respond by return and reassure me that you have not taken this heinous step!

Yours as ever,
Emma Woodhouse

My dearest Jane,

Still no word from you. I cannot easily bear this silence for I fear it means my letters have not reached you, that you have succumbed to the offices of your cousin, that you are married and have taken yourself to the further reaches of India, there to put aside your own passions in the service of one who does not, and cannot warrant your love and regard.

Are you indeed now Mrs St John Rivers? My dear Jane, you cannot know how that thought chills me. We scarcely know each other, and yet you have revealed yourself to me in such earnest terms that I cannot but care for you as a sister. And as a sister, I beseech you to ease my disquiet with all haste.

I would add only that I have spoken of you to Mr Knightley, and he is now of a mind to encourage my association with you. Please know also that our doors at Hartfield will always be open to you.

Yours, with all affection,
Emma

My dear Jane,

Alas, I fear this shall be my last letter to you for I have no notion that my words are reaching you, and I must put you out of my thoughts. I have news of my own which I would readily share, but I must await word of you.

Yours, with all affection,
Emma

My dear Miss Woodhouse, Emma!

Pray, forgive my silence, for much has happened during the last several weeks. I have your letters, forwarded by my dear cousin, Diana, from Moor House.

I will acquaint you immediately of my situation so that you may put your mind to rest. I am no longer Miss Jane Eyre, but the name which appends to me is not that of my cousin, Mr St John Rivers. Indeed, he is gone to India alone, and will no doubt do very well indeed.

Rather, I am Mrs Edward Rochester, of Ferndean Manor in the county of Yorkshire. You cannot know with what joy I impart this information, and lest you think ill of me, let me quickly explain. Soon after my departure from Thornfield Hall, the house was subject to a devastating fire, which all but destroyed it. Mr Rochester's erstwhile wife, Bertha, was responsible for starting the conflagration. She was a woman ravaged by mental illness, and cannot have known what her actions would bring. Mr Rochester tried to save her, as he saved all his servants, but it was not to be. Mrs Rochester, as though to deny her husband even that solace, flung her arms wide and leapt from the parapet, to be smashed on the pavement below.

Mr Rochester, Edward, escaped with his life, but left behind his sight, and one hand. As you may imagine he came close to losing his sanity also, but the spirits were on his side and he and I were reunited, though by what means I can scarcely tell.

My dearest Emma, I will indeed travel to Hartfield when I can be spared, but in the meanwhile, please share your news with all haste!

I am, dearest Emma, sincerely yours,
Jane Rochester

Heathcliff versus Sherlock Holmes

Bill Broady

On a first date it is always a good sign when you start rowing.

We began in a pub in Haworth Village. In what was presum-ably an attempt to spoof the tourists, its walls were lined with images and memorabilia of Brontë relatives who, although ignored by posterity, had led surprisingly eventful lives. There was Doc Brontë, the consumptive gunfighter, plugging his fellow players over a disputed poker pot: he appeared to have shot all three simultaneously. A case below displayed one of his six-guns, silver and remarkably tiny – almost like a child's toy. Then there was Bing Brontë, the once-celebrated crooner, seated in a canoe, serenading Dorothy Lamour with a ukulele. He looked even more malevolent than Doc. I wondered how many hapless Americans had fallen for all this – although, who knows, perhaps the tales were true?

There was Wolfgang Amadeus Brontë, his cloudy wig crowned with laurel leaves, next to the dying Admiral Horatio Brontë, French-kissing a startled Captain Hardy. In pride of place, above the spitting fire, was a shrine to Sherlock Brontë, The Great Detective, depicted wrestling with Moriarty at

The Reichenbach Falls, above a well-cured opium pipe and a chipped and stringless violin.

'That's an insult,' said my companion. 'Holmes beats The Brontës hands down.'

This display was the nearest we would come to Brontëana, for The Parsonage Museum was closed for renovation.

'The museum at 221B, Baker Street', she said haughtily, 'is open all year, except for Christmas Day.'

'But Sherlock Holmes never lived there,' I objected, 'or anywhere else, for that matter, being a fictional character. It should really be called The Conan Doyle Museum.'

'Who's he?' Having finished her wine she took a swig of my beer. 'It tastes like washing-up water,' she said, in a curiously approving tone. She remained adamant that Holmes was a real person, whereas Cathy and Heathcliff, with a little help from their friend Jane Eyre, had somehow created The Brontës.

'I'd like you to have seen it though,' I persisted. 'You could close your fists around Charlotte's tiny shoes. Those sisters were the size of dolls but they kept these enormous dogs, Keeper and Grasper. The last time I visited, the place was empty until there was this thundering noise, like horses flee-ing an earthquake, and thirty Japanese came running in. "Ah!" yelled their leader, pointing with her regulation duck-handled umbrella at a great brass ring in the vitrine next to me. "Keep-er collar!" Then they all kowtowed: maybe the Brontë pets are part of Shinto now? And there's Emily's beautiful watercol-our of her tame hawk, Hero. It's a sad story: when she came back from Brussels she found that her family had got rid of it. She scoured the fells but never saw Hero again.'

'You've just saved me seven quid,' she said. 'I don't need to go there now.'

We had met three days earlier at Salts Mill. As I sat in the diner, struggling with the *TLS* crossword, I became aware that a woman a few tables away was staring at me. Her long dark hair was elaborately coiled and stacked: although it was a

Wednesday morning in November she was all painted up as if for Mardi Gras. She came over and asked for the pepper and salt although all she had on her table was a cup of coffee, then walked back very slowly. She was dressed in a sort of bondage/beekeeping style with alternating layers of swathings and ligatures. Five minutes later, when she returned the unused condiments, she sat straight down.

'He's crap, Hockney, isn't he?' She gestured at the gaudy daubs that lined the walls, 'Although that Dufy-ish one might do for a beach-wrap.'

She had been working in London, in fashion, she told me, but had just moved up north to open a new boutique in Harrogate.

My dad would have called her hard-bitten. The face was like a mask but a regular subcutaneous ripple suggested that some biting was still going on. The eyes were large, dark and hypnotic: it was a while before I registered that they never blinked.

When we arranged to meet again I warned her to dress for wet weather and rough terrain but when she made her entrance in the pub she was wearing four-inch stiletto heels and a shin-length red wool coat over a tight cream angora sweater and brown leather hipsters vectored with Aero zips, leaving a gap to reveal an expanse of tanned stomach and back. Her passion for Sherlock explained the russet and grey checked deerstalker which had initially seemed a curious way to top off her ensemble.

We went outside. The clouds took one look at her and descended.

'It's a long way to Brontë Falls and Top Withens,' I said, but she indignantly declined my offer of waterproofs and gaiters.

'I've been up Croagh Patrick in these,' she said, lapsing into an Irish accent.

I persuaded her to compromise: we drove a couple of miles and parked up beyond Stanbury.

'So which is your favourite Holmes story?' – We were trudging up the bridle path that joins The Pennine Way.

'*The Hound of the Baskervilles*, of course.'

'You interest me very much, Mr Holmes. Would you have any objection to my running my finger along your parietal fissure? It is not my intention to be fulsome but I confess that I covet your skull.'

She stared at me blankly. 'Oh, is that in the book? I haven't actually read it but I've seen all the films, even the ones with Dud and Pete and Doctor Who. I've seen the one where Watson is really Holmes and Holmes is Moriarty and the one where they're gay and the one where they're both thirteen years old. But I like it best when it's not been messed about too much – when you can see Holmes thinking, when you can go inside his head.'

'I suspect that Robert Downey Jr may be a factor here.'

'Not really.' She scowled. 'He's nice but he's a bit too full of himself. You remind me of him.'

'Robert Downey Jr isn't bald.'

'Silly' – she reached over and slapped my pate. God, how I hate that clave-like sound! – 'I meant your voice.'

The sheep were out – grey and striated among the rocks, perfectly camouflaged against long-extinct predators. A cropping gimmer had petrified when we reached it, while a millstone grit boulder abruptly trotted away. The fog was thickening but there was no losing the path, lined with pale gravel, running between raised banks of heather and gorse.

'Now is the dramatic moment of fate, Watson, when you hear a step upon the stair which is walking into your life and you know not whether for good or ill.'

'That's a book line,' she said. 'Not a real one. In a film all you'd need to say is "Arrgh! The hound! The hound!"'

She walked with her left arm outstretched, as if there was a handrail at one side. It seemed to work: while my trionic Zamberlans slipped and squelched, she remained serenely upright on her two little spikes. I noticed that, on her wrist, the tiny watch face was obscured by condensation. 'It's always wrong anyway,' she said. 'It's an heirloom.'

The fog grew worse. It was quite impervious to the wind. If you stared at a patch for long enough it began to turn from grey to shell-pink. It was depositing yellow-green foam on our clothes. 'It looks like your horrible beer' – she licked her fingers – 'and it tastes like it too.'

We were continually startling invisible grouse which rose with whirring wings and rattling cries. 'G'day, g'day, g'day,' she replied. 'It's like being back in bloody Queensland!'

When we reached The Falls we could only hear them. We couldn't even see the narrow bridge beneath our feet.

'I'm sure we've already passed that funny-looking stone. Haven't you got a compass and a map?'

'Trust me, baby,' I growled, 'I know these moors.' If only I really could get lost!

'Do you get the feeling that we're being followed?'

'No, I think we're on the trail of something.'

She was relieved to discover a signpost of oddly translucent pine but the directions were in Japanese.

'I know the language a bit,' she said. 'Is there such a place as Hebden Bridge?'

'It's ten miles away, beyond the reservoirs. What does the other branch say?'

'Yokohama,' she replied.

We began to climb and the gale veered to blast directly into our faces.

'"Pure, bracing ventilation",' I shouted, '"they must have up there at all times, indeed; one may guess the power of the north wind blowing over the edge, by the excessive slant of a few stunted firs at the end of the house; and by a range of gaunt thorns all stretching their limbs one way, as if craving alms of the sun." That's the start of *Wuthering Heights*.'

'I must admit that I don't reckon much to The Brontës – at least, not compared to Sherlock.'

'I suppose you haven't read them either.'

'I don't like books,' she said. 'Why don't they make them smaller, so they'll fit into your bag? I've got a Kindle, of course, but I haven't downloaded anything yet.'

'Try *Shirley*,' I suggested. 'Lots of action.'

'I don't think so,' – she bridled – 'Shirley was my sister's name. And I DO know *Wuthering Heights*, thank you very much! I've seen the black and white one and the one with Voldemort and the one with James Bond. And I know *Jane Eyre* too – the old one with that fat man who used to advertise lager and the newest one with that cross-eyed girl who usually plays serial killers. They were all really boring but at least you could see what was going on.'

'I'm afraid I missed most of those. I would recommend Buñuel's *Abismos de pasión* or Rivette's *Hurlevent*.'

'Why would anyone want to bother with foreign versions of British things?'

'It's funny, I should have thought that most women would go for Heathcliff over Holmes. He's dark, enigmatic, brooding, dangerous and all that sort of stuff, whereas Sherlock is pale, sarcastic and querulous and even a little bit camp.'

'You obviously don't know women' – her elbow dug me in the ribs – 'or at least you've known the wrong sort. And just ask yourself one question: if Holmes and Heathcliff had a fight which would win?'

'It's not as simple as *Alien vs. Predator*, you know.'

She stopped, then stepped in front of me.

'I hope you don't mind me asking,' she said in an ominous tone, 'but what is someone like you doing round here?'

'I was born Round Here,' I said. 'Where do you think I should be?'

'I can't figure out why you go stamping around pretending to be all Heathcliffy when every inch of you just screams NW3.'

'I do love London and I did use to live in Belsize Park but try as I might I couldn't write a line there. Ah, sweet inspiration! – Round Here is where all my bodies are buried.'

The wind had dropped and we became aware of a hollow throbbing sound.

'Why is a helicopter up on a day like this?'

'It must be the wind turbines along the ridge.'

'I hate those things. Why will they never go round in sync?'

Her clothes had remained dry. Even with its flaps down she still contrived to look positively winsome in that ridiculous hat. She had left her coat unfastened but did not appear to feel the cold. I was muddied up to the knees but her shoes and trousers were immaculate. The next time I went a-wallowing across Great Shunner or Buckden Pike, I decided, I would wear white tie and tails.

She watched appreciatively as I extracted my right leg from a claggy hole: 'I like it when people are running from the hound only to be sucked down by quicksand instead.'

'You don't get quicksand on a moor. It's a BOG – The Great Grimpen Mire, to be precise.'

'You always have to be right, don't you?' She spoke witheringly, as if she had already lived through a lifetime of such moments.

'No, I just like to call things by their rightful names.'

'You're what the Germans call "ein besserwisser". Mr Know-All – that's YOUR rightful name.'

'What do you want me to do? Talk rubbish about subjects I know absolutely nothing about?'

'Why not? Everybody else does. You need to relax – stop trying so hard: life isn't an examination, you know.'

'But that's exactly what it is.'

'So who's going to judge us all, then? God?'

'No' – I struck a Zarathustra-like pose then strode boldly on – 'I will... seeing that no one else seems to want to do the job.'

We descended only to climb again, more steeply. The rain set in and I pulled up my wired hood.

'Top Withens,' I announced at last, reaching out to tap a hanging slab of mossy stone.

'How can you tell?'

'Because it's the only thing between Yokohama and Hebden Bridge.'

At these words she started back with a cry of what seemed genuine terror. A mephitic smell assailed my nostrils and I turned to find that a large sheep had sprung up on to the crumbling wall behind us. Even by the standards of West Riding blackfaces, it was a particularly disreputable-looking beast. The matted fleece was peeling off its belly and something about its expression – at once threatening and pleading – reminded me of Olivier playing Archie Rice.

'"Never in the delirious dream of a disordered brain could anything more savage, more appalling, more hellish be conceived than that dark form and savage face which broke upon us out of the wall of fog."'

'Do you remember everything you've ever read?'

'No,' I said, 'only the things I liked.'

'Look at its eyes! It's a demon!'

'All sheep's eyes are like that.' I rubbed my hand along its stubbly jaw. It had probably been hand-reared because it showed no fear. A green Dymo name tag – DYSON – had been punched into its ear. 'You can't have a demon called Dyson.'

'I'm sure that I met Satan once' – her eyes were wider than ever, with a curious lambent glow – 'and he swore that his name was Smith.'

The sheep, scenting no food, mooched back into the murk.

'Don't you ever blink?' I asked.

'I was dropped on my head as a child and for six months my eyes wouldn't close. Even now they sometimes click open when I'm fast asleep. People think I'm dead.'

She removed her deerstalker and let the cascade of shining black hair cover her face. Then, with one hand, she threw it straight back over her brow: how many hours of practice at the mirror lay behind such a gesture? Her face turned sideways and tilted, then appeared to detach itself to float across the space between us until we were kissing.

Her lips locked on to mine with remarkable suction but her tongue remained more reticent, dabbing away like the tip of a soft paintbrush. Her mouth did not taste of wine and cheese-and-onion crisps but of mouthwash and toothpaste, even though she had not visited the lavatory before we left the pub. It was like kissing a dental assistant – which had always been a fantasy of mine, sadly frustrated by my teeth being so healthy. All they had ever needed was a brisk scale and polish.

Suddenly she broke off, eyes rolling, giving that curious wail again.

Sheep Dyson had returned. Jaws clacking like a faulty loom, it was munching on the deerstalker, the chinstrap and brim of which, it appeared, had already been consumed.

'You knew it was going to do that, didn't you?' she spluttered, when we had finally stopped laughing.

'Yes' – the hat had completely disappeared and the creature now stood with one foreleg raised as if waiting for applause – 'it's what usually happens.'

The Curate's Wife – A Fantasy

Felicity Skelton

There was no possibility of taking a walk that day. I had been
wandering, indeed, in the leafless shrubbery an hour in the
morning… the cold winter wind had brought with it clouds
so sombre, and a rain so penetrating, that only the maid had
ventured further than the vegetable garden.

It was a house empty of any but the servants; my father was
away at synod. Bessie had offended me by re-ordering the pages I had been working on, and then withdrew to the kitchen
to sulk. When, an hour before supper, the rain stopped, and a
pale sun glistened weakly from just above the western hills, I
drew on my warmest coat and a woollen cap and slipped out
to exercise my frustrated limbs, and let the cool air into my
lungs and into my blood.

I climbed the hill by the usual path, a way worn by sheep
rather than man, and headed along the ridge in the dusk, making for the dip between the hill and Longlow; just below stood
the disused shepherd's hut that had become so often my retreat from the aggravations of domestic life. I had at one time
climbed up and replaced slates on the roof, so that it remained

a dry place where I could sit and read or write in solitude. In my pocket I carried my note-book, in which were the beginnings of a poem I wished to work on, and tucked inside was also the latest letter from my suitor, my father's curate. I intended to read it in private, and then leave it in the old tobacco tin in the wall where I kept all treasures which I did not wish anyone, let alone my father, to find.

As I took the few steps down from the ridge, my boots lost their grip on the wet scrubgrass. I slid inelegantly the few feet to the hut, and landed, breathless, hard against the stone wall. I heard a movement inside the building and was momentarily afraid, but I recollected my wits and stood, gingerly, peeping cautiously in through the gap in the stones where once there had been a window.

A man was crouched on his haunches over a small fire, the smoke from which I could now smell, though it had not been visible from outside in the damp evening air. He seemed to be wearing a greatcoat, which he had gathered about him; the collar was pulled up to protect the back of his head. For a moment I fancied he might be a large animal, or a rock, rolled in there in the storm a few days past. But no animal or rock could have lit the little heap of smouldering twigs and dry bracken on the muddy floor.

Emboldened, partly by the cold, and deciding that this was no tramp, I made my way to the doorway. The man sprang up as I approached, and faced me, his hand on the pocket of his coat, which I guessed held a pistol, or a knife. His figure was enveloped in a military greatcoat with large brass buttons, fur collared and steel clasped; where there had once hung epaulettes these had been removed, with some violence, as I guessed from the threads which still hung forlornly from the shoulders. He wore no medals, no decoration of any kind. The details were not apparent, but I traced in him the general points of middle height and considerable breadth of chest. He had a dark face, with stern features and a heavy brow;

his eyes and gathered eyebrows looked ireful and thwarted just now; he was past youth, but had not reached middle-age; perhaps he might be thirty-five. I felt no fear of him, and but little shyness. Had he been a handsome, heroic-looking young gentleman, I should not have dared to stand thus.

'You wish me leave?' he said, after a moment's pause, in which we regarded each other with some caution, as you may imagine.

His accent was not English, and I wondered whether he was perhaps Romany, although dressed rather too well against the weather. The cloth from which his clothes had been cut was heavy and the tailoring good.

'What do you do here, sir?' I asked, having decided that I had some rights in the matter. The moor might not be mine, but it certainly was not his.

'I am resting, mam'selle,' he responded. Now I had his nationality; he was clearly from France. But how or why a French military officer should be appearing in the wilds of northern Yorkshire was beyond my reasoning.

'You are far from home. Do you have food?'

'I have bread, *merci*.'

'And where are you headed?'

'I prefer not to answer.'

'I may be able to set you on the right road. You will find some people around here not greatly favouring your country-men. Many have lost sons or brothers in the wars with Napoleon. You will need to take care.'

He smiled.

'This, I think, I do. But I hope, mam'selle, that you have no such loss?'

'Not my family, no, thank God. But I grieve for others' loss, and for the French mothers, too, who have lost sons.'

He regarded me for some while without speaking, and I fancied his cheek blushed a little. This may be hindsight rather than a truth. It is hard, now, to recall what I knew then, since I have come to learn so much in the months since our meeting.

'*Asseyez-vous, s'il vous plaît,*' he said suddenly, as if remembering that he spoke to a woman. He moved aside, and revealed a saddle-bag, evidently carrying a heavy load, which lay folded behind the fire.

Now that it was almost dark, I was tempted to take advantage of the meagre warmth afforded by the miserable embers which still glowed on the floor, and I confess I was intrigued still as to who this Frenchman could be, and what might be his errand in the country. Against my conscience, it must be said, I seated myself, and held out my hands to the smouldering cinders, which with the judicious adding of further twigs and bracken collected from the corners of the hut, and a judicious kick from a well-worn military boot, sprang into life. My companion crouched again, and seemed to fall into something of a reverie.

By the light of the flames, which had caught on the dry grasses, I could now see his face more clearly. Something about his features seemed familiar, as if revealed in a dream, or in a portrait. And then I knew who this was, although still not how he could be here, so far from where I knew he should be. Whether I could admit my revelation without endangering my life, I was not yet sure, but my heart was beating so fast that I felt I might fall forwards onto the fire. As I steadied myself, he looked up.

'You are warm now? You should perhaps go?'

His gaze seemed to penetrate my mind and read my thoughts, and I did most earnestly begin to fear for my life. However, after we had regarded each other in silence for a few moments, his features softened, and I realized he was smiling at me, as if at a child who had said or done something amusing.

'Why are you here?' I asked, and my voice seemed to vibrate strangely in the enclosed space.

'I go to Scotland,' he replied, 'where I think they may have a place for me in their hearts.'

'What makes you say so?'

'The king over the water!' he said, raising an imaginary glass. '*La Vieille Alliance.*'

'And from there you plan to attack us?'

'No – I plan to live a quiet life. Maybe to have a family and a life like others have…?'

His eyes gleamed in the firelight, and I felt the power of this man, who was once so feared, but who was now believed to be under guard and in exile.

'How did you escape your imprisonment on the island?'

He paused before he answered me, perhaps considering how I had recognized him, and whether it would now be safe to allow me to go at all. Still, I was not afraid.

'I had friends, mam'selle.'

'But we have heard nothing here. You must have travelled for some weeks to get this far.'

'Days, only. I repeat, I have friends.'

'And in England?'

'Ah yes, indeed. You must know, there are some who would emulate the French, who would like a different system, a different governance.'

'Revolution, you mean? Like the Luddites?'

'They will not succeed. A pity, but they are not strong enough. But they have their sympathies…'

'They are thugs and murderers.'

'They fight for their dignity. It is simple. Would you not fight, if your life was to be intolerable? I think you are a fighter, too.'

I was silent, then, thinking over what my future might become. If I married Arthur, and behaved as a wife should behave, it would be the end to my writing, no more time alone, no more rambling the moors. I had fought, in my fashion, to stay free of servitude. I had known a life of disregard, when all that was available to me was drudgery and dreams. And if I refused to marry? I was past the age at which most single women have already become resigned to caring for some elderly relative – for me it would be my father – and when he was gone, I should live alone in some poor cottage, for I should have to leave the house where I had grown up and written my stories. The thought sprang into my mind, suddenly, that I had a story here which I could never tell, for no one would believe me, and if they did... I regarded the visitor with a new sense of my responsibilities. Again, his head had drooped, and he seemed almost asleep.

'You are tired,' I said. 'I will leave you to rest.'

As I began to rise, he took hold of my arm. His hand was warm, even through my coat, and strong. I stumbled, and fell to the floor beside him.

'I am not sure, mam'selle, whether I can allow you to go. I think, perhaps, you must stay until I am ready to move on. When I am rested, I can move fast, and your countrymen will not catch me. I am not called the Little Corsican for no reason. My island is mountains, and your English hills will not be obstacle to me.'

He rose, and lifted the old wooden door back into the doorway. It had been many years since the hinges had rotted through, and it leaned against the wall. I saw that there were lengths of wood which had fallen from it.

'You could put those on the fire, then,' I said. 'Let us at least be warm.'

I cannot now say why I had no fear of him. Perhaps I felt that, had he wanted to murder me, he would have done it by now. Perhaps I was already feeling something else for this man, whose French accent reminded me a little of another man I had once regarded highly. I know now that I am ashamed of what occurred, what I allowed myself to feel, and what I willingly did that night. For some days afterwards, I tried to believe that I had no choice, but the truth is different. This man could not have become ruler of an empire without impressing his character and his will on those around him. And he had charm, and notoriety, and a brooding countenance, which betrayed a thoughtful mind.

I had in my apron two or three apples, some of the last windfalls, and a hastily stolen chunk of Bessie's cheese from the pantry.

'Where is your bread?' I asked, spreading the supplies on the leather bag. 'We can make a half decent supper with these, if you have enough.'

'You are like a small lion,' he said. 'What is this?' He snatched up the letter from Arthur, which I now saw had fallen from my pocket.

'It is private,' I said. 'Please return it.'

He laughed and held it high as I reached for it.

'Ah – you have a lover. This is very interesting.' Seeing my flaming cheeks, he returned it, saying softly, 'It is yours, mam'selle, as he is yours. He is a fortunate man.'

'He is not my lover!' I said, indignant. 'He wishes to be, but I –' There was no good way to end this speech, and I was silent.

'I think you may be revolutionary, too,' he said. 'Your king had better take care, for I think you too do not wish to be ruled. I hear that he is, in any case, a madman.'

'I think he is not well. But the Regent carries out his duties as ruler. And I am quite content to be ruled by proper authority, there by the Grace of –' But here I stopped. To mention God in this company, in this close confinement, to this man, seemed somehow sacrilegious. I tried to think of a different subject, more appropriate.

'Revolution seems to me always to be the death of law,' I said. 'And the weakest are bound to suffer first.'

'That can be true. But without sacrifice, what can be gained?'

'You say that! You, an emperor!'

'Ah!' He was silent, and I thought perhaps he was reflecting on how far he had fallen in the ranks of men.

'Your country also killed her king,' he said, at last.

'And the people suffered.'

[121]

'So you are happy with everything the way it is? You think that the people do not suffer now? You do not suffer?'

I was silent for, of course, I knew that people in the village suffered, the farmers were struggling, I knew of poverty and cruelty and injustice. You cannot be the daughter of a parish priest, and visit the homes of the poor, and not know that sometimes life seems unjust. The local mill owners worked their hands hard, and many of them grew ill from the dust and the lack of proper food while the owners grew fat.

'And your own case?' he went on. 'Do you wish to be married to this man?' He gestured to the letter, which lay in my lap.

'I have not yet decided,' I said, at last. 'But I have little choice, if I am to have a comfortable home when my father dies.'

'*Exactement.*'

'And a revolution would help women escape from – that?'

'It is possible. Perhaps not immediately. Perhaps there are more important things to do first.'

'And when so many of a country's people serve against their will? Their talents disregarded, their place pre-ordained by the accident of their sex?' I had not known, until I spoke, just how strong was my despair.

He shrugged.

'There are many whose life is not what they would wish, and by the accident of their birth.'

This was incontrovertible, as I well knew.

'And does any revolution succeed? I mean, in bringing peace and contentment? Preventing disease and starvation?'

'That, too, may be possible. It is true, that in France, we failed to find an – *équilibre. Mais*, but, without the attempt, nothing can be won.'

We began to eat. He cut the cheese and his loaf of rough bread into pieces with the knife he took now from the pocket of his greatcoat, while I found handfuls of dry material to build the fire once more.

'You will not be missed?' he asked, gently, as I seated myself again beside him.

'It is our housekeeper's night off. She will have left out some cold meat for me. You could…' I stopped, for I was about to ask him back to the house, offer him a bed for the night and the means of washing himself. But this was too preposterous, and I decided, instead, to remain with him in the alien world of the shepherd's hut. Here was an adventure that I could never share with anyone, not even – perhaps especially not – with Ellen.

When we had eaten, and talked some more about his future, and my past, and I had told him of my successes as a writer, and promised that if he could let me know his address in Scotland I would send him copies of my books to read, the fire had burnt down and it was getting more difficult to keep warm. Involuntarily, I shivered, and he moved closer, and wrapped one edge of his coat around me.

'Keep warm, my little bird,' he said. I found my head drooping onto his broad breast, and though I knew that what I was doing was terribly wrong, I felt that I was no longer in a world that I recognized, where all was hedged around with restraint and propriety.

I need not tell you, dear reader, how the night went on. But since I know that I shall not last many more days on this earth, and that I and the baby that I carry are destined to stand before God within a short while, I must now set straight the record of my life, and the reasons I married when I had refused twice, and hope that in his heart Arthur may one day be able, with the aid of prayer, to forgive me.

Contributors' Notes

A. J. Ashworth (editor) is from Lancashire and is the author of the short story collection *Somewhere Else, or Even Here* which won Salt Publishing's Scott Prize and was published by them in 2011. The book was nominated for the Frank O'Connor International Short Story Award and shortlisted in the Edge Hill Prize. She is the recipient of a K. Blundell Trust Award from The Society of Authors for her novel-in-progress.

Elizabeth Baines is the author of a collection of short stories, *Balancing on the Edge of the World*, and two novels, *Too Many Magpies* and *The Birth Machine*, all published by Salt. She is also a prizewinning playwright for radio and stage.

Bill Broady is the author of two novels – *Swimmer* (2000) and *Eternity is Temporary* (2006). His short story collection, *In This Block There Lives A Slag*, won the 2002 Macmillan/PEN prize. With Jane Metcalfe he edited *You Are Here: The 'Redbeck' Book of Contemporary British Short Stories* (2006). His new novel, *The Night-Soil Men*, will be published next year.

David Constantine, born 1944 in Salford, Lancashire, was for thirty years a university teacher of German language and literature. He has published several volumes of poetry (most recently – 2009 – *Nine Fathom Deep*); also a novel, *Davies* (1985), and four collections of short stories: *Back at the Spike* (1994), *Under the Dam* (2005), *The Shieling* (2009) and *Tea at the Midland* (2012). He is an editor and translator of Hölderlin, Goethe, Kleist and Brecht. His translation of Goethe's *Faust, Part I* was published by Penguin in 2005; *Part II* in 2009. OUP published his translation of the *The Sorrows of Young Werther* in 2012. He was the winner of the 2010 BBC National Short Story Award and the 2013 Frank O'Connor International Short Story Award. With his wife Helen he edited *Modern Poetry in Translation*, 2003-12.

Carys Davies's short fiction has been broadcast on BBC Radio 4 and published by *The Dublin Review, Granta New Writing, The London Magazine, Prospect, The Royal Society of Literature Review, The Stinging Fly* and various anthologies. She was the winner of the 2011 Royal Society of Literature's V. S. Pritchett Prize and the 2010 Society of Authors' Olive Cook Short Story Award. Her first collection *Some New Ambush* (Salt, 2007) was longlisted for the Wales Book of the Year, shortlisted for the Roland Mathias Prize and a finalist for the Calvino Prize in the US. She was the winner of a 2013 Northern Writers' Award for the development of her second collection of short stories. She lives in Lancaster.

Sarah Dobbs' novel *Killing Daniel* was published by Unthank Books in 2012. She has a PhD in Creative Writing from Lancaster University and currently teaches at Edge Hill. In the past she has won a Funds for Women Graduates Grant and co-founded Creative Writing the Artist's Way, where she mentors writers. You can follow her on Twitter @sarahjanedobbs

Vanessa Gebbie is a Welsh writer living in Sussex. She is author of two collections of short fiction, *Words from a Glass Bubble* and *Storm Warning – Echoes of Conflict* (both Salt Publishing), and contributing editor of the creative writing text book *Short Circuit, Guide to the Art of the Short Story* (also from Salt). Her novel *The Coward's Tale* (Bloomsbury) was chosen as a *Financial Times* Book of the Year. She writes poetry, was awarded the 2012 Troubadour International Poetry Prize, and her debut pamphlet *The Half-life of Fathers* is published in 2013 by the Sussex-based Pighog Press. She also teaches widely. www.vanessagebbie.com

Tania Hershman is the author of two story collections: *My Mother Was An Upright Piano: Fictions* (Tangent Books, 2012), a collection of 56 very short fictions, and *The White Road and Other Stories* (Salt, 2008; commended, 2009 Orange Award for New Writers). She is writer-in-residence in Bristol University's Science Faculty and editor of *The Short Review*, the online journal spotlighting short story collections and their authors. Tania teaches regularly and gives workshops on short stories, flash fiction and science-inspired fiction. www.taniahershman.com

Zoë King is a freelance writer, editor and creative writing tutor who lives and works in Norfolk. In another life, she was editor of *Cadenza* short fiction and poetry magazine. Her short stories have been published across the world, and she has won a number of competition prizes. She currently chairs the Society of Women Writers & Journalists (www.swwj.co.uk). Her own website is at www.zoeking.com

Rowena Macdonald was born on the Isle of Wight in 1974, grew up in the West Midlands and now lives in London. Her first book, *Smoked Meat*, was published by Flambard Press and shortlisted for the 2012 Edge Hill Prize.

Alison Moore's first novel, *The Lighthouse*, was shortlisted for the Man Booker Prize 2012, in the New Writer of the Year category of the National Book Awards 2012, and won the McKitterick Prize 2013. Her debut collection, *The Pre-War*

House and Other Stories, was nominated for the Frank O'Connor International Short Story Award 2013. Born in Manchester in 1971, she lives near Nottingham with her husband Dan and son Arthur. www.alison-moore.com

David Rose was born in 1949; he spent his working life in the Post Office. His novel *Vault* was published by Salt in 2011 and his short story collection *Posthumous Stories* will be published by them in 2013.

Felicity Skelton is a writer of short stories and poetry, and lectures in English and Creative Writing at Sheffield Hallam University. Her story 'Geography' is in *Overheard: Stories for Reading Aloud*, edited by Jonathan Taylor (Salt, 2012). She is currently researching contemporary Canadian short fiction for a doctoral thesis. A collection of stories, *Eating A Sandwich*, was published by Smith/Doorstop in 1999. She has also contributed to books on fiction and pedagogy, and had short stories published in *Mslexia*, *The North*, *Sheffield Thursday* and *Sheaf*. She had a previous career as a professional theatre director.

Inspirations

Elizabeth Baines:

Many women have said to me that as teenagers they identified, as I did, with Cathy in *Wuthering Heights*. I started reading the Brontës when I was ten or eleven, and through my teenage years I read *Jane Eyre* and *Wuthering Heights* several times. However, being a pretty tempestuous teenager myself, it was with the passionate and wilful Cathy and her intense and doomed relationship with Heathcliff that I came most to identify. I did notice that the homely housekeeper Nelly Dean, who relates the story to new tenant Lockwood, sometimes expresses disapproval of Cathy's behaviour and attitudes, but I found that no obstacle whatsoever: I was very much used to being in trouble with adults, whom I saw with self-righteous rage as just *wrong*.

The book's structure of multiple frames and contrasting viewpoints has strongly influenced me as a writer, but until I read it again recently I had never questioned my teenage notion that Nelly's homeliness and disapproval (and the somewhat wispy and straight-seeming Lockwood who retells Nelly's tale for the reader) were set up merely as ironic counterpoint to the true, rightful heart of the story, the young couple's passion and their perspective.

Reading the book again not so long ago, I saw that I – and the many films of the book, and indeed critics down the years – had been wrong. The self-absorption of the Cathy-Heathcliff relationship wreaks havoc for those around them, especially the next generation. The younger Cathy is born unnoticed and 'unwelcomed' in the midst of her mother's deathbed obsession with Heathcliff. The book doesn't end with the elder Cathy's death (as some film versions do), but goes on to chart how the younger Cathy and her cousin Hareton must deal with their legacy of subordination to the self-centred, self-consuming passions of an earlier generation, and a more concrete disinheritance at the hands of a passionately yet coldly vengeful Heathcliff. Hareton and the younger Cathy do survive, and they do so by learning, unlike either Heathcliff or the elder Cathy, to be reasonable.

In other words, *Wuthering Heights* isn't the romantic or gothic book many of us have taken it to be. Rather, it's a book *about* the romantic or gothic impulse – romantic obsession, wilful submission to violence and death – and its dangers. Yet, as Joyce Carol Oates points out in her essay, 'The Magnanimity of Wuthering Heights' (*Critical Inquiry*, Winter 1983), the striking – and brilliant – thing about the novel is that, while chiefly concerned with those dangers, it nevertheless takes us into the *experience* and the attraction of that romantic/gothic impulse, enabling us to identify with the elder Cathy and Heathcliff even as it shows their error.

Still, I would say that my identification with the elder Cathy probably influenced my behaviour and attitudes as a teenager, and other women have told me the same. It was this, and my more recent realization, that inspired my story, 'That Turbulent Stillness'.

Bill Broady:

Grateful acknowledgements to Helen G. and Sally C. but –
above all – to Sheep D.

David Constantine:

I read *Wuthering Heights* yet again and was most affected this
time by the claustrophobic violence of it and by the idyll of
Catherine and Hareton reading together at the end. But my
story also has in it the moors to the east of Manchester that
I loved and walked on as a boy and have gone back to again
and again: their closeness to the city, the unspeakable cruelty
they were the location of in the 1960s. My story is a sort
of utopian answering back against that cruelty. It has to be
read for itself, as a bid for love, pity and kindness. But it is
haunted by the knowledge of what adults may inflict upon
the children.

Carys Davies:

Charlotte Brontë's publisher George Smith was charming,
handsome, clever and eight years younger than she was. He

became her good friend and frequent correspondent and attentive host when she visited London. Brontë biographers and scholars have long speculated on what the true nature of their relationship might have been. To me, based on the available facts, it seems probable rather than merely possible that Charlotte was in love with him and that he knew it; against the background of Charlotte's tragic family history, her desperate loneliness and sense of personal inadequacy, it is one of the most poignant stories of unrequited love I've ever come across.

In my imagination, the fictional encounter depicted in 'Bonnet' takes place towards the end of 1853, when – and these are the facts – Charlotte is thirty-seven and Smith is twenty-nine and has recently become engaged to Elizabeth Blakeway, the beautiful daughter of a wealthy London wine merchant, but no one, including Smith himself, has told Charlotte yet.

The historical truth is that Smith seems to have felt unable to break the news to Charlotte, prevaricating and writing to tell her, eventually, only after she has found it out from his mother. When she does, at last, receive his letter, Charlotte writes back what must be, as Brontë scholar Juliet Barker says, 'the most extraordinary letter of congratulation ever written'*:

My dear Sir

In great happiness, as in great grief – words of sympathy should be few. Accept my meed of congratulation – and believe me

Sincerely yours
C. Brontë

Charlotte married the Reverend Arthur Bell Nicholls, curate at Haworth, in June 1854. She died in March 1855 at the age of thirty-eight, probably of tuberculosis aggravated by acute morning sickness.

* *The Brontës: A Life in Letters.*

Sarah Dobbs:

'Behind all the Closed Doors' was written as an attempt to understand the grief that goes with losing a parent at such a young age. It's a nod to the bond of family, the ones that are here and those that aren't. In some small way, I hope it also shows the varied roles and importance that particular books can have for us.

Vanessa Gebbie:

The story 'Chapter XXXVIII – Conclusion (and a little bit of added cookery)' was a joy to write. The opening line of the final chapter of *Jane Eyre*, 'Reader, I married him,' is so iconic, and I was just wondering idly what would have happened to them all if Jane and Rochester did not marry after all. What would that final chapter contain? I started by turning everything that happened into its own negative – and the story took off when Mr Rochester developed a penchant for odd cooking and sacked his kitchen staff. What a liberty. What horrors. (But it was great fun to write and I hope it makes you giggle as much as its writer did when creating this slightly mad story.)

Tania Hershman:

I took all the first lines of all the Brontë novels and used them as prompts.

Zoë King:

The idea for 'My Dear Miss…' arose from an exercise I used with my writing class, in which they were alone in a well-stocked bookshop late at night, and privy to conversations between characters in any two books of their choice. The original idea morphed into a series of letters for me, and while Jane was always going to be the primary correspondent, several potential characters battled for the privilege of being the recipient. Some of them are still waiting in the wings…

Rowena Macdonald:

'A Child of Pleasure' was inspired by the relationship between Lucy Snowe and Ginevra Fanshawe in *Villette*. Ginevra is a hilariously awful character, who is extraordinarily rude to Lucy but also wants her friendship. I found the scenes between them the most compelling in the novel, partly because I don't understand why Lucy puts up with Ginevra with such forbearance but also because, although Lucy is the proto-feminist, Ginevra struck me as a very modern character type: immodest, narcissistic, shallow, concerned mostly with money and appearance: the kind of woman who wants to be the star of her own social circle, a wannabe 'celeb' 150 years before celebrity culture existed.

Alison Moore:

'Stonecrop' was inspired by a line from *Wuthering Heights*: 'After all, she was a sweet little girl.' When the first line suggested itself to me, the story followed.

David Rose:

'Brontësaurus' is based on an acquaintance, sadly long dead, whose retirement project was just such a concordance to Emily Brontë's poetry. That, however, was long before the internet, when a search engine was a wettened finger. All details in the story are therefore fictitious.

Felicity Skelton:

The idea for 'The Curate's Wife' has been knocking around in the back of my head for many years. I loved the Brontës, Charlotte in particular, even when I was very young, and read several biographies as a teenager. Of the books, the favourite has always been *Jane Eyre*, particularly for the bits that people don't talk about so much: Rochester dressed as a gypsy, Jane's weird paintings. It wasn't until I sat down to write the story for this anthology that I realized there was only one way to start it, and only one way to describe the mysterious figure in the shepherd's hut. I hope Charlotte doesn't mind my theft, nor my playing fast and loose with the historical facts.